## Other Books by Elizabeth Maddrey

Peacock Hill Romance Series
*A Heart Restored*
*A Heart Reclaimed (Spring 2018)*

Arcadia Valley Romance – Baxter Family Bakery Series
*Loaves & Wishes* (in *Romance Grows in Arcadia Valley*)
*Muffins & Moonbeams*
*Cookies & Candlelight*
*Donuts & Daydreams*

The 'Operation Romance' Series
*Operation Mistletoe*
*Operation Valentine*
*Operation Fireworks*
*Operation Back-to-School*

The 'Taste of Romance' Series
*A Splash of Substance*
*A Pinch of Promise*
*A Dash of Daring*
*A Handful of Hope*
*A Tidbit of Trust*

The 'Grant Us Grace' Series
*Joint Venture*
*Wisdom to Know*
*Courage to Change*
*Serenity to Accept*

The 'Remnants' Series:
*Faith Departed*
*Hope Deferred*
*Love Defined*

Stand alone novellas
*Kinsale Kisses: An Irish Romance*

For the most recent listing of all my books, please visit my website.

.

*For Valerie Comer*
*Thanks for inviting me to be a part of Arcadia Valley.*
*And more for being such an amazing friend.*

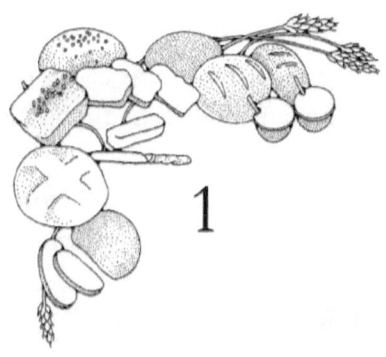

# 1

"Oh, thank goodness you're still open." Jonah Baxter pulled the door to Page Turners closed behind him.

A young woman with almost orange hair looked up with a smile, slipped a bookmark between the pages, and laid her novel on the counter. "For about another hour. Last-minute shopping?"

Jonah blew out a breath. "Yeah. The season kind of got away from me. I'm Jonah Baxter. I don't think we've met?"

"Kenia Akers." She gestured to the shelves of books that filled the store. "Can I help you find something?"

He dug in his pocket and drew out a crumpled piece of paper that he unfolded and tried to smooth. "I have a list. Sort of."

"That's a start. Let me see it." She snagged the paper from his fingers and frowned. "What kind of paper is this?"

Heat crawled up his neck. "Parchment paper. My brothers and I run A Slice of Heaven Bakery. It's what was handy. Malachi does all the business stuff and he gets testy if I raid his desk—says I mess up his organization."

"It has a nice texture." She rubbed it between her fingers. "What's it for?"

"Lining pans. To keep cookies from sticking, that sort of thing. You've never used parchment paper? These days it seems like everyone watches cooking shows and knows all about the tools of the trade."

"The kitchen isn't really my favorite place to be." Kenia shrugged. "I think we have all of these. Eclectic list though."

"My siblings have mixed taste."

"You're all readers?"

He nodded. Reading was something his parents had prized and the love of it had been learned as little children, cuddled up on the couch while his mom and dad took turns reading aloud. They'd traveled as a family through Narnia and Middle Earth, and had joined the other farm animals in their amazement at Charlotte's web designs. As they'd gotten older, most families quit reading aloud together. Not his. They'd gone to the center of the earth and the deepest, darkest parts of the sea, then surfaced and walked through the Lake District of England with Lizzie Bennett and pondered philosophy couched in the story of four Russian brothers. Even as adults, before his parents died, evenings when they were back home ended with a chapter or two from whatever Mom and Dad were reading together. "It's a family passion."

"I like that. Flowers are my family's passion, primarily. But we do like books."

"That's good, seeing as you work in a bookstore."

Kenia laughed. It was a strong, friendly sound. "Very true. Here," she pulled a thick hard cover from one of the shelves, "who's this one for?"

"Malachi. He and his wife Ursula are both addicted to this fantasy series, but I know they're a couple of books behind, so hopefully they don't have the latest already." Jonah frowned. What if they did? "What's your return policy like?"

"I'll get you gift receipts. They can exchange it if they need to." Kenia moved down the shelves, consulting his list periodically and pulling out books. He could've done it himself. Wandering a bookstore was a nice way to spend an hour or two. Then again, following behind someone with as nice a figure as Kenia wasn't exactly a hardship.

"If you're busy, I can get the rest."

"We're almost done, and it's not as if we're packed."

He chuckled. Most people probably did their shopping well ahead of Christmas Eve. He'd meant to do all his shopping online last week, but they'd been slammed with orders for Christmas parties and family gatherings, and it had slipped his mind. When he'd gotten home from the bakery, he'd wanted nothing more than a hot shower, an hour of quiet, and bed. "I appreciate it."

"Who's Ruth?"

"My sister. You've probably met her, Ruth DeWitt? She runs the Fairview Bed and Breakfast. She loves to shop here."

"Of course. That means you and I have probably met—or at least seen each other—at Grace Fellowship."

He nodded. That would explain the nagging feeling that he knew her.

"And who's Serena?"

"Soon-to-be sister-in-law."

"Your wife or girlfriend doesn't like to read?"

Jonah shook his head. He'd thought about getting something for Gloria. Not that she was his girlfriend. In fact, she'd made it very clear that she was *not*. They were friends. Maybe friends rated a Christmas gift, but he hadn't wanted it to seem like he was pushing. "No wife. No girlfriend."

"Really?" There was a glint of something in her eye. It couldn't be interest, could it?

"What about you? Do you get your sweetheart books for Christmas?"

Pink tinged her cheeks. "I'm not currently involved."

Hard to imagine. She was cute and spunky. In fact, she reminded him of Gloria a little. They didn't share any physical resemblance, but their personalities were similar.

Kenia cleared her throat. "Okay, I think that's everything, unless your list is missing someone?"

Jonah set the stack of books on the counter and mentally ticked through the recipients. "Nope, that's everyone. I really appreciate it."

"That's what we're here for." She rang up the books and told him the total. Jonah managed not to wince as he handed her his credit card. Maybe he should've gone for paperbacks, but that seemed too cheap for Christmas.

"It was nice to meet you, Kenia." Jonah hefted the two bags of books and aimed for the door. "Merry Christmas."

"Gee, what'd you get us, Jonah?" Micah laughed as he came from the kitchen into the living room. It was nice of Corban to let the two of them continue to share the family farmhouse. Well, for one more week. After that, it was just going to be Jonah rattling around in here by himself. Ruth and Corban as well as Malachi and Ursula still stopped by to spend the evening. A lot. But it wasn't the same.

"I still have the receipt." Jonah glowered at his brother and finished stacking the last book under the tree. "You're lucky I got you anything for Christmas since I have to get you a wedding present next week, too."

Micah beamed. "You do, don't you."

"Yeah, yeah." Jonah shook his head. It didn't really bother him. Much. Was it ever going to be his turn?

"So, what'd you get Gloria?"

"Nothing."

"Come on. Christmas is tomorrow, I'm hardly going to spill the beans between now and then."

"I'm serious. I didn't get her anything. We're just friends. You don't have to get friends a Christmas gift."

Micah snorted. "Yeah, you do. Especially when you're half in love with her."

"I'm not." He couldn't help sounding defensive, and it was obvious his brother heard it, too.

"You keep telling yourself that."

He would. Over and over again until it finally stuck. Gloria had been clear. Multiple times.

"You need to get her *something*."

Jonah rubbed the back of his neck. "I guess I could go online and get her a gift card."

Micah sighed. "You're pathetic."

Probably. But it didn't change the fact that, against the yearnings of his heart, he was trying to respect Gloria's wishes. They were friends. Nothing more. "What am I supposed to do at almost nine p.m. on Christmas Eve?"

"Go online and get her a gift card. I just don't understand why you didn't get her a gift before now."

"What'd you get Serena?" It was time—past time—to change the subject.

"You're going to think it's stupid."

"No, I won't." Or, at least, he'd try to keep from laughing in his brother's presence.

"There's this new kiln she's been eyeing. But she keeps talking herself out of it because she doesn't really need another one. But this one has some bells and whistles her existing kilns don't have. So...it seemed like it'd be worthwhile. She can do some new techniques with it."

"That's not stupid, that's thoughtful. And expensive."

Micah shrugged. "Yeah, a little. But I have some savings, and since her parents are insisting on paying for the wedding, and her dad sent me a check that he said I had to use for at least part of our honeymoon, I figured it was worth the splurge."

"You okay with that? The money?"

"I am. Now. Her parents' hearts are in the right place. They have the money and they like to spend it on the people they love. It's just been a little bit of an adjustment. And I don't want to get used to it, you know? I mean, Serena could decide this is the last movie she's ever going to do. And we'd be okay with our income from the bakery and her potting."

Jonah laughed. He'd seen the unrestrained joy on Serena's face on her occasional breaks from filming or in the photos Micah took when he zipped out for a weekend to see her. She wasn't quitting acting anytime soon. But still, it was a good thought.

"So. Gloria?" Micah dropped down on the couch and leaned his elbows on his knees. "Is she not going to be your plus one at the wedding next week?"

Jonah sighed. "I want her to be."

"Have you asked her?"

"Not yet."

"Why not?" The look on Micah's face said he clearly thought Jonah was an idiot.

Jonah hunched his shoulders. "I get tired of being shot down. I've been asking her out for two and a half years. She'll come to the bakery every day and flirt. She'll come to family gatherings or outings with big groups and only hang out with me. But when I ask her out on something that can't possibly be defined as anything other than a date, I get an instant no and the reminder that she's not looking for a relationship."

"I thought maybe she'd eased up on that since she's been coming to dinner so often."

"That's just to see Serena, I think." Jonah shrugged. "Maybe I'll just go stag."

"Don't be silly. Ask Gloria. Since Mal's the best man and Gloria's the maid of honor, it's not like they're going to pair up beyond the recessional. Plus, you're paired with Ursula, so Mal's going to want her back. And Corban isn't going to relinquish Ruth. Ever. So since you're the only two unattached people in the wedding party, you might as well go together."

"I guess. I'd planned to just leave it be. Since she's so dead-set against relationships, it's not like she'll be bringing anyone anyway. So we'll hang out and that'll be fine." At least, that seemed like it would be the case. The woman drove him crazy. His brother wasn't wrong about being half in love with her, no matter how much he denied it when asked. But it all seemed rather hopeless.

Micah frowned. "Ask her. If she matters to you, give her another chance."

Jonah nodded. One more chance. And then? Then he was going to work on getting her out of his system for good. There was only so much rejection he could take.

"Merry Christmas." Gloria strolled through the doors of the bakery holding a wrapped gift in her uniformed arms.

Jonah chuckled and set aside the paperback thriller Ruth had given him as part of his Christmas gift. "You're a day late."

"And a dollar short."

"In that case, the coffee's on the house." He stood and crossed to the coffee station. "The usual?"

"Sure. What's the cookie today?"

"Peppermint chip. They've been a big hit all December. But I tried something else out, if you're feeling adventurous?" Jonah set one full mug of coffee aside and filled a second for himself. He added a generous splash of agave to Gloria's coffee before dumping half and half in his own.

Gloria sat at one of the small cafe tables and set the present in front of her. "I'm always game to be a guinea pig."

"Cool. One sec." He set the coffees down on the table and pushed through the swinging door that led to the kitchen. He pressed a hand to his racing heart. How, after nearly three years, did she still have this effect on him? Especially when she wanted nothing more from him than friendship? When would he get a clue?

Using tongs, he loaded four orange spice donuts onto a plate. He glanced over to where he'd hung his coat this morning. The gift card he'd printed online Christmas Eve after Micah hounded him was in the pocket. But...she had an actual present. He groaned and dug out the envelope he'd slipped it into. At least he had *something* to give her. He grabbed the plate and headed back out in the front of the bakery. "Here we are."

"Ooh. Those look pretty. What kind?" She reached for a donut and sniffed it. "Orange?"

"It's sort of a riff on wassail. Orange and clove and some other Christmassy spices. The guys thought they tasted good. So have the handful of customers who've been in today."

"Slow day?" She bit into the treat and her eyebrows lifted. "Mmm. This is good."

He grinned, his insides warming at her approval. She'd been on his mind while he was mixing the flavors. Gloria exuded that warm, comforting aura he always associated with wassail. He'd added a little bit of ginger and extra clove to bump up the spice. Gloria had that bite, too. "Glad you like them. As for slow." He shrugged. "I can't complain. I thought about closing the rest of the week, too, but we didn't get nearly as many vacation holds as I was expecting on the weekly orders, so it made sense to come in and get people their bread and treats. We have some big orders for New Year's parties, too."

"And you're making Micah's cake?"

"Yeah. The party orders all have to be picked up or delivered by tomorrow. That still gives me two days to get the cake squared away."

"So you're only open two days this week?"

He nodded.

"That's good. You deserve a little break. You work hard."

"This from the lady who spent her Christmas patrolling the streets of Arcadia Valley."

"Yeah, well, I'm a cop. Without family. I might as well take my turn so someone who'll benefit can have the day off. Speaking of that, though. I brought your gift." Gloria pushed the wrapped rectangle across the table.

"Thanks. I got you this." Jonah tugged the envelope out of his pocket and handed it to her. He was probably supposed to open the thing...but it was already better than what he'd gotten her simply because it was a real gift.

"When I saw that, I thought of you and knew you needed it. And if you already have it, I can return it."

He took a deep breath and tore the paper, revealing the latest cookbook by one of his favorite chefs. He'd eyed it at the bookstore when he was shopping for gifts on Christmas Eve, but had held off in case someone got it for him. When none of his siblings did, he'd planned to get it himself later this week. His fingers itched to snatch the gift card out of her hand. "I don't have it yet. I've been wanting it, though. Thanks."

Gloria opened the envelope, her eyes dimming as she pulled the printed gift card out. "Oh. Nice. Thanks."

He winced. "I wasn't sure...I mean...I don't usually get things for friends. You know what? Let me get you something else."

"No, this is fine. It's great. Really." She tucked the paper into the breast pocket of her uniform and emptied her coffee. "I guess I should get back out there."

"Let me grab you a box for the other donuts." He stood, his gaze falling on the cookbook. Maybe she did care. "Gloria? Would you be my date for Micah's wedding?"

She pressed her lips together and there was a frantic edge to the way she shook her head. "No. Jonah...we're just friends. That's all we can ever be. I'm sorry. I...I have to go."

Jonah's heart sank as he watched her flee the bakery. That was the last time he was listening to his brother when it came to dating. Jonah might be half in love with Gloria, but that was his problem. He'd get over it—over her. Eventually.

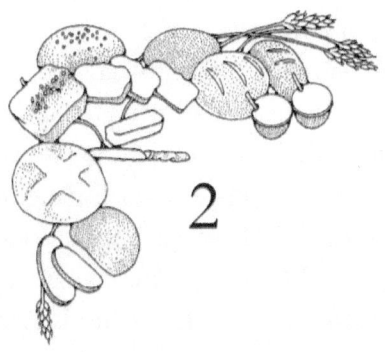

2

Gloria rang the doorbell and tucked her hands in her pockets. She heard kids hollering inside the house and smiled in spite of the heaviness of her heart.

Constance Espinoza, the wife of her fellow police officer, pulled open the door with a broad grin. "Gloria! What a nice surprise. Come in out of the cold."

"Thanks, Constance." Gloria stepped in and pulled off her gloves, stuffing them in the pockets of her coat. She unwound the scarf from around her neck. "Is Felipe around?"

"Of course. He's back in the den. Let me take your things. Can I bring in some coffee? Maybe some cookies?"

"I don't want to impose..."

"Nonsense. I'll be right in. You go. And if Ava's in there trying to convince her dad to give her more chocolate, send her out to me, would you? It's time for us to read and get her ready for bed." Constance folded Gloria's coat over her arm.

"Thanks." Gloria wiped her feet on the mat inside the door. Should she take off her shoes? They weren't super wet and she didn't plan to stay long, might as well keep them on. She headed down the hall to the kitchen and turned in to the den. Felipe was parked in a leather recliner, sock-clad feet up, his small daughter in his lap. The picture on the TV flickered, but the sound was off.

"No, Ava. I'm pretty sure mama wouldn't go for that." Felipe kissed his daughter's head. "Isn't it bedtime for you?"

"You put me to bed?"

Felipe kicked the recliner closed and started to stand, pausing as his gaze landed on Gloria. "Looks like I have company. I think it's mama's turn tonight."

Ava's lower lip poked out. "But I want you."

"I know, *Corazon*. I'll check in on you later. Go read and get ready for bed." He kissed her again and gave her a little swat on the bottom to get her moving before grinning at Gloria and putting his feet back up. "Did you just finish work?"

Gloria nodded.

Felipe gave her a long, measuring look. "What brings you out tonight?"

Gloria rubbed her damp palms on her jeans. "I was hoping you had a few minutes to talk. I...need some advice. But if you want to put Ava to bed, I can wait."

"No, it is good. Constance loves to read with the girls. Have a seat. What's on your mind?" He reached for the remote and switched off the TV completely.

Where did she even start? She settled into the second recliner but leaned forward, clasping her hands. Felipe knew her history. He was one of the few people in Arcadia Valley who knew all of it. "Jonah asked me to go to his brother's wedding."

Felipe frowned. "Aren't you in the wedding?"

"Yeah. Serena's one of my best friends. But all the other attendants are married. To each other. Jonah and I are the only single people. I guess he thought it made sense for us to pair up, too."

"Hmm. And you said no."

Gloria sighed. "Like I've said no every time he's asked me out for the last two years."

"He's persistent."

She smiled weakly. "I guess."

"Why does he keep asking? It is odd, isn't it, for a guy to do that when the lady in question has made it clear she's not interested?"

Her cheeks warmed. "I'm not completely sure I made it clear. We're friends. Good friends."

Felipe nodded. "I see."

Constance came in with a tray. She slid it onto the end table between the two recliners. "Coffee. Decaf, so don't worry. And some cookies the older girls helped me make this afternoon. They might need to be dunked in the coffee."

"Thanks, *mi alma*."

"Yeah, thanks. I'll try not to be much longer."

"Please. You're always welcome here, you know that. And when Felipe takes time off, he misses the job, so it's good you came and can fill him in on what he's missing."

Gloria chuckled and watched as Constance left the room. "You're not missing anything. It's slow around town right now."

"Figured. That's why I went ahead and took the vacation time. Back to Jonah. You haven't told him?"

She shook her head. "I haven't told anyone in so long...I don't even know how to work it into conversation. And until Jonah came to town, it wasn't an issue."

Felipe sipped his coffee contemplatively. "The way I see it, you have three options. One, you can let things keep on the way they are. At some point, he will give up and move on. I'm guessing that'll be sooner than later. Two, you can tell him you're already married. That should get him to stop asking you out. Or, three, you can track down your no-good husband and file for divorce."

"I can't...I made those vows. I meant them." Her heart ached. She didn't love the man she'd married anymore. They'd been apart for too many years. She didn't even know if he was alive. And with the way he'd been living when he kicked her out, it was a real possibility that he wasn't. Still, she wasn't going to be the one to end things. The way she read the Bible, she owed it to him to be willing to try to reconcile. Maybe at some point her faithfulness would lead him to Jesus.

Felipe sighed. "I still think you've given him more time than anyone would require. You've been here what, eight years now?"

"About that."

"What will you do?"

"You really think Jonah will give up?"

"I would have a long time ago."

Gloria reached for a cookie. "I guess I'll wait a little longer. Before I could tell Jonah, I'd need to tell a lot of other people first. It feels like opening Pandora's box."

"I'd consider it lancing a boil. But I won't push. Yet."

"Thanks."

He shrugged. "I'm not sure I did anything. But let me say one last thing?"

"Okay?"

"Jesus said it best in John eight—the truth will set you free."

Gloria nodded, her stomach clenching. Maybe he was right. Maybe that was the better, smarter, course of action. But she couldn't go there. Not yet.

At her apartment, Gloria changed into sweats and her Marine Corps sweatshirt. She only wore it around the house. Not many people knew she'd served for four years before coming to Arcadia Valley to be a cop. For that matter, none of her life before Arcadia Valley was widely known. She wandered into the second bedroom that she used primarily for storage, though she had vague plans of turning it into a study someday. So far, that had translated into some cheap bookshelves on one wall and stacks of boxes on the other. She'd lived here going on nine years and still lived like this was a temporary stop.

She hefted the only box that sat alone on the floor and carried it into her bedroom. Sitting cross legged on her bed, she took a deep breath and lifted the lid. Gloria fought a sneeze at the puff of dust and gently lifted out the uniform cap and set it aside. Underneath was the certificate she'd received at her promotion to sergeant. She managed a slight smile as she set it next to the cap. There it was.

Swallowing the lump that formed in her throat, she took the photo album from the box and placed it in her lap. She hadn't opened it in almost five years. Was this walk down memory lane really necessary? Before she could talk herself out of it, she opened the cover and blinked back the tears that filled her eyes as her gaze landed on her wedding photo.

She and Frank both looked sharp in their dress uniforms. They'd met at Parris Island, trained together, sweated together, complained together, and somewhere in there, forged a friendship. After graduation, when they both ended up heading to the Military Police Basic Course, that friendship slowly morphed into love. When they'd finished school, they'd taken weekend liberty and found a Justice of the Peace to make it official.

Gloria sighed and turned the page. She traced her finger over photos of their first apartment together but skipped over the postcards and letters he'd sent when he'd been away on temporary duty. More pages flipped and the brief happy period of the marriage was over—they just hadn't known it yet.

Deployment was hard on marriages where one spouse was a civilian. But when both spouses got deployed to different places it had to be a little worse. They were both in harm's way and schedules never aligned, so even if she'd had a chance to call or link up with him online, he was rarely free.

And then he'd been injured.

She'd gotten emergency leave to see him in the hospital. But then she'd had to go back overseas, while he'd been shipped home for recovery. And while he was getting used to his prosthesis, Gloria had learned the value of prayer and, thanks to the Chaplain, found Jesus. Then, finally, she'd gotten to go home, only to discover that Frank had found an addiction to pain killers and Darla. Maybe Marla? The woman's name wasn't important, but she symbolized the end of everything.

Gloria snapped the photo album shut and tossed it aside. She peered into the box. There were a handful of letters, most were missives she'd sent that had been returned unopened. Brushing an errant tear off her cheek, she loaded the memories in the box and settled the lid on. Maybe Felipe was right. Maybe it was time to take action and end things.

Her phone rang and she pushed the box to the end of the bed as she checked the caller ID. Serena. Gloria forced a smile as she answered. "Hey."

"Hey, yourself." Serena's voice was full of enough pep to power a small country. "Five more days!"

"You ready? It's not like you were sitting around while you were planning this thing. I'm not even sure *how* you plan a wedding while you're filming a movie." Gloria tucked the phone between her ear and her shoulder and scooted off the bed. She grabbed the box and carried it to the other room. Better to leave it there, out of sight. Maybe in time, she could get it out of mind as well.

"I think we are. The only thing left is the cake, and Jonah assures me he has that under control."

Gloria frowned. "I guess he's had practice twice now."

"Yeah. Though I'm not sure how he'll manage to be *groom* and baker some day. Maybe he'll go ahead and contract that one out." Serena paused before clearing her throat. "Do you have a plus one you need to tell me about?"

Gloria huffed out a breath. "No."

"Okay. Just asking. Thought maybe you might have ended up needing to sit with someone..."

"Fishing like this is unattractive. Jonah asked me. I said no. I thought—hoped, even—that you'd at least understand." Gloria pressed her hands to her eyes. Did she just need to explain the whole sordid mess to the world to make them understand? Her stomach twisted. She couldn't. It was humiliating. And heartbreaking. She didn't want to deal with everyone's pitying glances and conversations that tiptoed around any topic that might relate to marriage.

"I'm sorry. I'm trying. But...I don't get it. The two of you are great friends. You hang out all the time when the family gets together or if there's something going on at church. You stop by the bakery practically every day and flirt with him. So what's the deal?"

"I don't flirt."

"Girl, you do."

No. She didn't. "We talk. Banter, maybe. But it's not flirting. Unless you're saying I flirt with the guys on the force, too?"

"Maybe you do?"

"No. I'm just one of the guys. It's how we talk. I can't help it that Jonah doesn't understand that. I've been as clear as I can."

"I still say you have feelings for him. Tell me I'm wrong."

She couldn't. But she also couldn't have those feelings. Shouldn't. Wouldn't. She might not love the man she was married to, but she could choose not to fall in love with someone else. "I can't. But it doesn't matter. There's no chance for us, Serena. Could you please let it go?"

Serena sighed. "I want you to be happy."

"Not everyone gets a fairytale ending. Besides, it's not like I'm some gorgeous Hollywood starlet. I'm just a cop who's more at home in jeans and work shoes than a skirt and blouse. Speaking of that..."

"Nope. You have to wear the dress. A fancy pantsuit is not the same thing. Besides, you look amazing in it."

"Says who?" Gloria winced. "Never mind. Don't tell me. I can guess. I'll wear it. But I draw the line at heels."

"Fine. Wear the ballet flats. Can I still seat you near Jonah, even though you're not officially going together? We decided not to have the whole bridal party at one table. Micah and I will have a little round table just for us, the rest of you will get scattered around."

That was better than being up at a head table on display. But sitting with Jonah...would be fun, provided he could just be a friend. "Okay. Now, what do you need me to do between now and the wedding? I have a little time."

"I'll text you a list. Thanks."

"You got it. Micah tell you where you're going on your honeymoon yet?"

Serena laughed. "Nope. He's keeping that close to the vest. I'm sure it's going to be great. Are you okay?"

"Of course I am. Text me that list. 'Night." Gloria ended the call and let her shoulders slump. Maybe she should've said yes to Jonah. Would that have been wrong? They could go as friends, couldn't they? They'd done that for lots of things over the last two years. Somehow, a wedding was different. Maybe it was knowing how he felt about her that changed things? Maybe it was understanding that she felt the same way.

Even though she knew she shouldn't.

Gloria pushed through the door of A Slice of Heaven and breathed in the heady scent of yeast and sugar that permeated the air. A hint of coffee wound through, accenting the aroma, and making her mouth water. Her gaze wandered down the glass display cases before coming to rest on Micah at the register. Her eyebrows lifted. Usually Jonah was out here when she stopped in.

"Hi, Gloria. What'll it be today?" Micah set his book aside and stood.

"Maybe I'll go for the cliché and get one of those chocolate frosted donuts and some coffee."

Micah chuckled. "Have you tried the apple spice?"

"You mean orange spice?"

He grinned. "Those were yesterday. We have apple today."

"Guess I'll be walking some of my patrol this afternoon. I'll have one of each. Did you have a good Christmas?"

"We did. I think Ruth was hoping you'd swing by after you got off work."

Guilt wormed its way through her. She'd thought about going, but it had been a long, boring day, and she hadn't been up for all the happy couples. With Jonah asking her to the wedding yesterday, she'd probably made the right choice. At least when he'd extended the invitation they'd been alone. If he'd asked in front of the whole crew she might not have been able to say no. "I didn't want to intrude. Christmas is a family thing."

"We consider you family." Micah's smile was gentle, offsetting the hint of chastisement in his voice. "I thought you knew that."

"I do. It's just..." She sighed and reached for the bag holding her donuts. "You know how complicated this is, don't you?"

Micah shrugged and punched buttons on the register. "Do you need a to-go cup or will you stay here?"

"I've got a few minutes if it won't bother you."

"Not at all." He took her money and dropped change in her palm. "Might even join you for a minute or two. I could use my afternoon jolt of caffeine."

Gloria nodded. She dropped the bag of donuts on one of the tables before carrying her mug to the coffee station and filling it. Clearly Micah wasn't going to volunteer any information about Jonah. Which meant she had to ask. "How's Jonah?"

Micah's eyebrows lifted. "About like you'd expect."

"So...he's fine?"

Micah just looked at her.

She hunched her shoulders and sipped the coffee. She really needed to figure out a way to budget beans from The Beanery into her life. The grounds in a tub from the grocery store couldn't hold a candle to the magic Grant Ward worked. At least she managed one cup of the good stuff a day. The sludge they passed off as coffee at the station might as well be tar. She cleared her throat. "I don't understand why he's surprised."

"I wouldn't say surprised. He wasn't going to ask you. I pushed him into it. I really didn't think you'd have a problem. I mean, you're the two unmarried members of the wedding party, it just makes sense."

Serena had said something along those lines last night. "And we're still going to end up sitting together from what Serena said last night. So what's the trouble?"

Micah frowned. "Are you really never going to date him? We're coming up on three years. That's a lot of flirting for nothing to come of it."

Gloria winced. They thought she was a tease. "I wasn't flirting. I was talking. But maybe it's best if I don't come by so often."

"Maybe it is." Micah stood with his coffee and shook his head. "I'm sorry."

"Yeah. Me, too." Gloria drained her mug and snatched the bag of donuts off the table before striding through the door back to her cruiser. At least she wasn't going to end up needing to walk in the biting wind that had just picked up to work off too many pastries. Her stomach was twisted into so many knots she couldn't eat if her life depended on it.

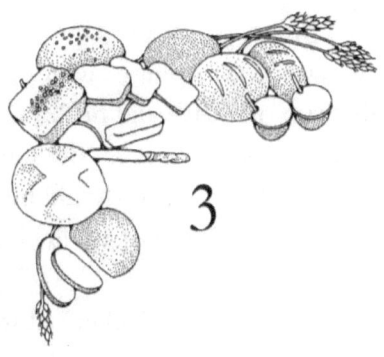

3

Jonah ran a knife around the edge of the cake pan and flipped it onto a cooling rack. With an expert twist, he lifted the pan off and inspected the layer. Not bad, if he said so himself. He peeled the parchment paper off the top and tossed it toward the trash can, smiling when it went in. Eight other layers joined this one to make three each of three different sizes. They were spread on the counter, cooling. He pressed fists into the small of his back and groaned. That was enough for today.

The cakes needed to cool completely before he could put them in the fridge. Since the shop wasn't open today—and wasn't that weird, being closed on a Saturday?—he'd cleaned everything while the cakes baked. Maybe he'd go for a walk.

Jonah checked that he had the key and his cell, made sure the ovens were off, and pulled the bakery door closed behind him before heading north toward town. It was cold—maybe the walk wasn't such a good idea—but at least it wasn't snowing. Yet. He tugged his black watch cap down over his ears and shoved his hands further into his pockets.

His boots crunched on the frozen sidewalk as he strode along. What was he doing? He should be back at the bakery with a cup of coffee and his book. Or he could go home and find some way to help with wedding preparations. Two days out, there should be plenty to do. Of course, the cake and other pastries he'd worked on all day *were* his part.

At Main Street he paused, checked for traffic, and hurried across the street. The lights in Page Turner's, the local bookstore, glowed yellow through the plate glass window. They were a beacon, drawing him closer, promising warmth. He didn't need another book. His siblings had all gotten him at least one for Christmas...but you couldn't really have too many books, could you?

He pulled open the door and the cheery jingle of bells seemed to welcome him. Jonah tugged off his cap and shoved it in the pocket of his coat before running a hand through his hair. That pretty girl—Kenia—wasn't behind the front desk. His heart sank and he frowned. Had he come here hoping to see her? That was...unexpected.

Unzipping his coat, he wiped his feet on the mat and sauntered between the shelves, letting his hand trail along the spines of the books as he browsed. Toward the back of the store he paused. She was up on a ladder, sliding books into place on the top shelves. She was wearing a sweater and a plaid skirt that brushed her knees and somehow she managed to look both scholarly and feminine at the same time.

He cleared his throat. "Hi."

Kenia turned, one hand gripping the ladder. "Oh." Her eyes brightened. "Hi. Jonah, right?"

"Yeah."

"Back for more?"

"I had a little break at the bakery—we're closed, but I'm working on a wedding cake—thought I'd go for a walk. Ended up here."

Her eyebrows lifted and a smile flirted with the corner of her mouth. "Can I help you find something?"

"I don't want to interrupt. Just thought I'd say hi. I can poke around on my own."

Kenia looked at the stack of books balanced on the rung of the ladder in front of her then back at him. "I'll be done in a few. I'll come find you."

He smiled and gave a short nod before turning and heading down another aisle of books. By the time she found him, he had a cookbook he'd been considering for a while now, the latest in a thriller series he and his brothers both enjoyed, and two first-in-series mysteries that sounded good.

"Guess you didn't need my help after all."

Jonah tapped the mysteries. "These any good?"

"People seem to like them."

He nodded. It wasn't a ringing personal endorsement, but maybe she wasn't a mystery reader. They weren't for everyone. Ruth couldn't abide them. She was romance and nothing but romance. He'd thought that was the case for women generally until he'd met Ursula. That girl could put away sci-fi books with the best of them. And it was unlikely she'd ever read anything that hinted of romance. "Got any recommendations?"

Kenia eyed the stack of books in his arms and nodded. "Come with me."

Jonah followed, trying not to notice the way her skirt swished around her knees. It wasn't as if she was trying to walk provocatively. He could—would—be a gentleman. Besides, she was probably too young for him. He'd be thirty-three before long and she had to be...younger.

She stopped in front of the thrillers and pulled a book from the bottom shelf. "Have you read this series?"

"No." Jonah took the book and flipped to the back to read the blurb. Hmm. He added it to the pile.

Kenia laughed. "That was easy."

"How old are you?" He cringed. "Sorry. Sometimes my mouth gets ahead of my brain."

Her eyebrows lifted. "I'm pretty sure you're not supposed to ask women that."

"Yeah. I have a sister. I know better. Forget it."

"No...I don't think so. Now I'm curious. Why do you ask?"

Heat warmed his face and he cast around for a plausible explanation. "Just wondering."

"Nope. Don't buy it."

He cleared his throat. "I'm nearly thirty-three. I was wondering how close—or far apart—in age we were."

"That wasn't so hard, was it?" She rested her fingers briefly on his arm and grinned. "Twenty-eight."

"You look a lot younger."

"I'll take that as a compliment."

He nodded. "It's how I meant it. So, you read thrillers?"

"I read books. Any kind. I think it'd probably be a bad idea to work in a book store if you didn't love the merchandise."

That made sense. It was why he had to be around food. He'd tried, for a while, to find a career that wasn't in the kitchen. That hadn't worked well. At all. The bakery was good. But he missed the fast pace of dinner service in a busy restaurant. All the ingredients and smells mixing together. The texture. The color. Something itched between his shoulders, but he knew from experience no amount of scratching would make it go away.

"What else do you like?" Kenia nodded at his stack.

"This pretty much covers it. I can put up with sci-fi and fantasy if it's recommended by one of my brothers, but otherwise." Jonah shrugged. "Not really my thing."

"Hm. What have you read?"

He squinted and came up with a couple of titles Micah had foisted on him over the last year.

Kenia grinned. "Those are good ones. You liked them?"

"They were okay."

"I have one or two others you should try sometime. When you finish with that pile, come see me again and I'll hook you up."

Had she winked? Her eyelid had flickered, but maybe that was a muscle spasm. Gloria had him so twisted up, he wasn't sure he'd recognize flirting if it came with sirens and a flashing light. Besides, it wasn't reasonable to assume a pretty girl like Kenia would see anything in him. Was it? But what if she did? If things were really and truly never going anywhere with Gloria—and that seemed to be the case—then...what did he have to lose? "Are you busy Monday night?"

"New Year's Eve?"

"That was dumb. Of course you are. I don't know what I was thinking." He clutched the books closer to his chest and started to turn. "I should get back to the bakery."

"Wait. I'm not doing anything important. Ben and Evelyn Kujak—do you know them?—they're having a party out at their place. My brother Grady and his wife and I think Alaina and Cameron will be there. Whole lot of couples. I was going to tag along because it beat hanging out with my parents, but I could be persuaded to change my plans. Easily."

"Would you want to come to my brother's wedding? I'm a groomsman, so you'd have to sit alone during the ceremony. Or you could just come to the reception?"

"Won't you be up at the head table?"

Jonah shook his head. "They aren't doing that. Just a couple's table. Everyone else will be spread around. So I can just let Micah know I have a date and it'll be fine. I can promise the desserts are going to taste good. And they got L'Aubergine to cater, so I'm guessing dinner will be fantastic, too."

"Count me in. That sounds like fun."

He grinned and let out a breath. "If you don't mind coming a little early, I can pick you up?"

"Even better."

Jonah mentally scrolled through the day's activities. He was going to leave the cake in the fridge at the bakery as long as possible, but it still needed to be set up at the country club before the ceremony. He just wouldn't have time to do it otherwise. Unless he took Morgan Taylor, the chef/owner of L'Aubergine, up on her offer to handle it. No. It was the cake. He'd do it himself. "Maybe four thirty?"

"I can do that. What time's the wedding?"

"Seven. It's dressy. I'll be in a tux, obviously, but I think some of the guys attending will probably wear them anyway." Jonah walked with Kenia toward the front of the store and set his books down on the counter. "Can I get your number, just in case?"

Laughter danced in her eyes and she held out her hand.

Jonah dug his phone out of his pocket, swiped it on and tapped for a new contact before handing it to her.

Kenia's fingers flew on the screen and, after a moment, her skirt pocket chimed. She handed back his phone with a grin. "And now I have yours. I texted my phone."

He nodded and set his credit card on top of the books. "I'm actually not dreading this wedding now."

She chuckled and rang up his purchase. "I'll take that as a compliment, too."

"It's how I meant it." He smiled and reached for his card and the bag of books. "Thanks. I'll see you Monday." Jonah bundled back up before stepping out into the cold. A few brave snowflakes were trying to fall, but the fact that he had a date kept him warm all the way back to the bakery.

Jonah escorted Gloria into the reception hall when their names were called. He glanced around for Kenia. She'd said she didn't mind finding their table and waiting there for him. The logistics of being in the wedding party and having a date who wasn't hadn't occurred to him, but the worst should be over now. "I'm going to go find my date. You're good, right?"

Gloria nodded. "Of course."

Jonah grinned and strode across the empty dance floor toward Kenia. She looked amazing. He needed to come up with a better adjective though. He'd used that one twice already. "Hey. Sorry."

"It's not a big deal."

"I think I'm done for the evening now. So that's something." He pulled out his chair and sat, surreptitiously wiping damp palms on his legs.

"It was a lovely wedding. And did you see who's here?" Kenia nodded toward the tables where Serena had seated her parents and Hollywood friends. "It's like a page out of a magazine."

Jonah chuckled. "I'll admit to having been a little star struck myself, though talking to them, they seem pretty normal."

"No way."

"It's true." He shrugged. "Micah says they're good people, but they kept the wedding smaller to limit who they could invite. And that's part of why they got married here instead of L.A. Serena didn't want the big circus. For a while, I figured they'd elope."

"Really? Could you do that? Elope?"

Jonah considered for a minute. "I don't see why not, under the right circumstances. Weddings are for making promises to one another and to God. The party isn't really necessary. Not that there's anything wrong with having the party, if you're sane about it."

"Define sane."

He looked around the silver and gold classic Hollywood themed space and pursed his lips. "Have a budget. Stick to it. That sort of thing. Micah wanted to pay for the reception, but Serena's parents insisted."

"Technically, that's their prerogative."

"True. But—" Jonah broke off as Gloria pulled out a chair at the table and set the place card with her name on it in front of her plate. "Hey."

Gloria's tight smile didn't reach her eyes. "Hi. I guess they figured since we knew each other we should sit at the same table."

Awkward. Jonah shifted in his seat. What was his brother thinking? "Have you met Kenia Akers? Kenia, this is Gloria Sinclair."

"You look really familiar. Do you shop at Page Turners?" Kenia shook Gloria's hand.

"I've been in a time or two, but you've probably seen me on patrol. I'm a cop?"

"Oh! That's it. It's nice to meet you. Don't you go to Grace, too?"

Gloria waggled a hand from side to side. "Sometimes. Sometimes I go to Arcadia Valley Community. Sometimes I'm working."

"Hey, Gloria. You look so lovely in that dress." Ursula, dragging Malachi by the hand, hurried to the table and dropped their name cards by two plates. Her gaze drifted to Jonah, then to Kenia, and back to Jonah. "Hi Jonah, looking dapper."

Jonah chuckled and stood as his sister-in-law took a seat. "I assume Mal's told you how nice you look?"

Ursula grinned and fluttered her eyelashes at her husband. "He has."

"Do you know Kenia?" Jonah stretched his arm around the back of Kenia's chair. "Kenia, this is my other brother, Malachi, and his wife, Ursula."

"Sure, hi. We've met at church a few times."

"And the bookstore." Malachi grinned. "I spend entirely too much money in there."

Kenia shook her head. "No such thing as too many books."

Everyone at the table laughed.

"You won't get many arguments from our family." Jonah brushed Kenia's shoulder with his fingertips. He looked across at his brother. "Did you see who else they put at our table? Are Ruth and Corban here, too?"

Malachi nodded. "They're working their way over. Ruth is putting up several of the Hollywood folks who came out, so she wanted to stop by and say hello, make sure they were taken care of. You know how she is."

Jonah nodded. Their sister was born to be an innkeeper. She enjoyed having people come in and out of her home, loved having the chance to chat and serve them. It would be interesting to see how she managed when the baby came. Last he'd heard, Ruth and Corban were closing for the month of April. That should give them a chance to settle in, at least a little, with the baby. After that? It was probably good he and his brothers were all close enough to pitch in when needed.

Ruth and Corban dropped their place cards on the table and Ruth eased into her seat with a groan.

"You okay, hon? Can I get you something?" Corban rested his hand on Ruth's shoulder, his face apprehensive.

"I'm fine. It's just a long time to stand in heels when you're five months pregnant." Ruth smiled. "Hi, Kenia. Did I know you were coming?"

Kenia glanced at Jonah and lifted her eyebrows.

"I think I mentioned it on Sunday." Jonah's hand curved around Kenia's shoulder. Out of the corner of his eye, he caught a grimace flit across Gloria's face. Was she not feeling well? That was the third time since she sat down.

The minister stood and tapped his water glass for attention. "Let's go ahead and bless the meal. Please bow your heads with me."

His prayer was brief, focused on the meal and the blessings of friendship and sharing in the celebration of a couple committed to God and to one another. After he closed, quiet music filled the room and servers in black and white began filtering through the room with trays. Everyone's place card listed their entree selection, so it was a relatively quick process to get everyone served.

Quiet conversation floated around the table. Kenia had plenty to say. She was definitely more talkative than Jonah had anticipated. It was nice. And, with the exception of Gloria, who still looked like she might be ill, Kenia was getting along well. If anything came of this date, it was good to know his siblings liked her. In a family as close as his, that mattered. A lot.

When the dishes had been put away and Micah and Serena had floated through their first dance, couples started to fill the empty space in the middle of the room.

Jonah glanced at Ruth. "I'm trying to picture Mom and Dad at a wedding with dancing."

Ruth laughed. "I've been trying to do that since Serena first mentioned the plan. At least there's no alcohol. I know that was a big issue with her family. Even this morning they were trying to get her to change her mind. They didn't think people would have a good time without it. Particularly on New Year's Eve."

"Did they decide on sparkling cider or sparkling grape juice for the midnight toast?" Jonah didn't particularly care which one. He liked them both.

"I think they're offering a choice." Ruth shrugged. "You should go dance. I know you enjoy it."

"What do you say, Kenia? Care for a turn around the floor?" Jonah held out his hand.

Kenia slipped her hand into his with a nod. "Sure."

Jonah spun her in a little twirl before pulling Kenia close. He'd taken dancing lessons several years ago. It was the only part of his relationship with Melissa that he didn't regret. It was good to be able to hold his own when the opportunity to dance arose.

"You're not bad at this." She laughed and slid her arm up his shoulder.

"Thanks. Same goes. Are you having fun?"

"I am. I'm glad you invited me."

He grinned. "I'm glad you said yes."

The evening passed quickly. Jonah and Kenia danced for much of the time, breaking now and then to rest, eat cake, and chat with the others at the reception. Periodically, Jonah looked for Gloria. She hadn't left the table. Should he ask her to dance? No. She'd been clear about their relationship, such as it was. And he had a date. It wouldn't be right to ditch Kenia just to try and help a friend have fun. For all he knew, Gloria *was* having fun.

So why was she glaring at him?

Pushing it out of his mind, he glanced at his watch. "Almost midnight."

"Let's find a seat. I could use that cider." Kenia fanned a hand in front of her face.

Jonah grinned. "Me, too. Looks like they've already set it out at the tables."

As the song came to an end, the D.J. picked up the mike. "If I could get everyone's attention? We're coming down to the countdown, so find that special someone and get ready to toast in the New Year. Everyone ready? Let's count it down."

The crowd of people at the tables and on the dance floor joined in the chant.

"10..9..8..7..6..5..4..3..2..1..Happy New Year!"

*Auld Lang Syne* started to play and Jonah leaned closer to Kenia, his eyes holding hers. "Happy New Year."

Her eyelids lowered.

Jonah's gaze darted to her mouth. It was their first date. Much too soon for a kiss. Except...he leaned in and brushed his lips across hers. "I think I read it's bad luck not to do that."

Cheeks pinking, Kenia giggled. "Well, we wouldn't want that."

Jonah tapped his glass of sparkling cider against Kenia's and sipped. There hadn't been fireworks, but as kisses went, it hadn't been awful. Maybe in time, it'd get better. His gaze darted to where Gloria sat frozen. She caught his eyes and stood, her chair toppling backward as she hurried into the crowd. He looked back at Kenia and forced a smile. "Another dance?"

"Absolutely."

"Hey." Ruth pushed open the farmhouse kitchen door and slid a covered casserole onto the table.

"Morning. I didn't expect to see you today." Jonah looked up from his book and reached for his coffee. In fact, he'd been anticipating a day with no human contact, a rare break from the bakery with nothing else planned. Probably best not to mention that, though. "What brings you over?"

"I don't have a lot of time. Most of the guests are still sleeping. Did you know the reception went until almost two, when management finally kicked everyone out?"

Jonah shook his head. "We left about twelve thirty. Kenia was starting to yawn."

"That's what I wanted to talk to you about."

"Oh?"

"A head's up would've been good. Did anyone know you were bringing a date?"

Jonah peeled up one corner of the foil on the casserole and smiled at the baked sausage and egg mixture inside. "Sure. I mentioned it to Micah. That's how Kenia had a place card."

"He didn't say anything?"

"Like what?" He stood and crossed to the cupboard where the plates were stored. Grabbing a fork on the way back to the table, he frowned at his sister. "What's the problem?"

"Gloria—"

"Didn't want to go with me. I did ask her first." Using the fork, Jonah dug out a generous piece of casserole and levered it onto his plate. It was cold, but that wasn't a problem. Not for him.

Ruth sighed and gestured to a chair. "Can I sit?"

"Of course. Want some of this? Or some coffee?"

Ruth pressed her lips together before nodding. "Yeah, sure. To both."

Jonah retrieved another plate, fork, and cup of coffee for his sister before returning to his own plate.

"She really said no?"

"Yep. Just like she's said no the last, oh, six hundred times I've asked her out. I'm done. I said I was done this summer, but now I really mean it. This time, I explained it would just be as friends—two people who knew each other, who were both in the wedding party, and who could hang out comfortably for the evening. She still said no."

"I'm sorry." Ruth chewed on her bottom lip before adding, "She seemed to regret it."

"How do you figure that?"

"You didn't see how she looked at you and Kenia?"

Jonah shrugged. "I figured she was grumpy. She gets that way sometimes. I've learned to roll with it."

Ruth sighed and put a small square of sausage and eggs on her plate. "I'm not convinced Kenia is the right girl for you."

"Seriously? She was your idea."

"What? Please."

He shook his head. "In August, when you announced your pregnancy? Dinner party? Any of this ringing a bell?"

"Not...rea—oh. Maybe? I thought you said she was too young?"

"Turns out, she's not as young as she looks."

"Lucky her." Ruth sipped her coffee, eyeing Jonah over the rim of her cup. "Are you serious about her?"

"That was our first date. I'll have to let you know. I'm thinking I'll ask her to do something on Friday. We can see how things go when we aren't at a wedding." Weddings weren't great first dates. At least, not in Jonah's mind. There was a lot of pressure for romance at a wedding. Maybe he should've gone by himself, but Gloria's continued rejection stung. It had been nice to be with someone who didn't seem to think spending time with him was a bad idea.

Ruth frowned and set her coffee down.

"What do you expect me to do? It's been nearly three years. Honestly? She could probably arrest me for stalking, if she wanted to. It's time to move on. Past time." And Kenia...well, she was a nice girl. Maybe there could be something between them, even if it wasn't the spine-tingling fireworks he'd always anticipated when he found the right woman.

"Every good love story starts with a certain amount of stalking." Ruth grinned and held up her hands before he could retort. "Okay, okay. I want you to be happy. I just...I want Gloria to be happy, too. She's such a good friend—to all of us."

He nodded. "She is a good friend, which is why I think I need to walk away and bury whatever feelings I have for her."

"What are those feelings?"

Jonah shook his head. He wasn't going to explore those with his sister. He barely spent time thinking about it when he was alone in his room, trying to fall asleep.

"You know feelings have names, right Jonah? And that it's okay to talk about them?"

He snickered. "I love you."

"I love you, too. You're okay then?"

"Yeah. I'll let you know if it changes."

"I'm going to hold you to that. I should probably get back to the B&B. Don't eat all those eggs in one sitting."

"Yes ma'am." He stood and offered her a hand. She took it and pulled, levering herself out of the chair with a groan. "Take care of my niece."

"Or nephew."

"Or nephew. Tell Corban if he wants to escape later, I'll probably have the game console on."

"Oh, no. He doesn't get to escape when we're booked solid. Nice try."

"Offer stands if you change your mind. Why didn't you drive? It's freezing out there."

Ruth shrugged and pulled the edges of her coat closer around her neck. "It's not that far. I'll text you when I'm home if you're worried."

"Do that. I don't need Corban finding you frozen solid in the cornfield."

Laughing, Ruth pulled the door closed behind her. Jonah watched as she scurried through the dormant fields toward the B&B.

Feelings. He had plenty of them for Gloria, and she wanted nothing to do with them. It was time to see if he could develop them for someone else. Someone who wanted them. All the experts said love was a choice. Jonah chose a woman who would choose him back.

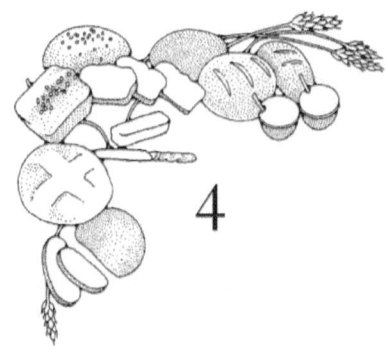

4

Gloria drove past the bakery, forcingherself not to stop. She hadn't spoken to a Baxter since the wedding on New Year's Eve. Almost two weeks ago, now, and it was like a part of her was missing. Couple that with Serena off on her honeymoon in Bimini and Gloria's off-shift time had been quiet. Lonely. Felipe had invited her over several times, but there was only so much imposing she could do. Besides, his big happy family was just that. Since she wasn't likely to ever have one of her own, it was hard to be around right now.

Her choice, of course, but that didn't make it any easier.

She hadn't been able to trade shifts with anyone or pick up an extra, which meant a long, solitary Friday night stretched out in front of her. Maybe she'd just go home and read. Except, of course, she needed a new book and right now, heading into Page Turners wasn't high on her list of options either. Was Jonah really dating Kenia? Her heart ached. This was what she wanted though. Of course it was. She'd made it clear he needed to move on and he finally had. That was good. It was. In time, her heart would catch up with her head.

It had to.

So. No bookstore, and it was too late for the library, which meant no new book. Which left the TV.

Ugh. Maybe she should bite the bullet and buy an e-reader. Then she could get books online whenever she wanted. It just seemed wrong to have to plug something in to be able to read. Books were a sensory experience. Or they should be. She didn't spend a lot of time reading, but when she did, it was because she wanted to unplug. Even if she did hop on the technology train, it didn't fix her prospects for tonight. She wasn't about to try to read on her phone.

Gloria turned her car into the apartment building parking lot and found a space. She sighed as she eyed the ramshackle structure. The landlord skirted on the edge of being a slum lord. Half the windows didn't have screens, the half that did weren't really winning the occupant any benefits, there was so much rust on them. But the place was cheap and she didn't have to spend off time doing yard work. What would she do with a house, anyway? It was just her. She practically rattled around in the two-bedroom apartment.

She climbed the stairs to her unit and frowned as she glanced down the hall. Someone was sitting against the wall opposite her door. Waiting for her? Who? Her hand went to her holster and she took a breath and forced her muscles to relax. Aiming for casual, she strolled down the hallway.

The man shifted and surged to his feet, tucking his hands in his pockets. "Hello, Gloria."

"Frank?"

He stepped into the glow the overhead light cast on the dingy hall carpet. She wouldn't have recognized him if he hadn't spoken. He was thin—bordering on emaciated—but his hair was clean and neat, as were his clothes. "Could we talk?"

She stared at him, her blood roaring in her ears. Finally, she nodded. "I guess you'd better come in."

Gloria unlocked her apartment and pushed open the door, gesturing for him to go ahead. She hadn't been thrilled about a long, lonely night but now? That sounded just about perfect.

"Thanks."

Movements jerky, Gloria closed the door and flipped the deadbolt out of habit. She tossed her keys into the bowl by the door—Serena had made it and it never failed to make her smile. Until tonight. Her stomach rumbled. She'd meant to stop by Fire and Brimstone to grab a pizza. Now...she wasn't going out in public with him. "I was going to scramble some eggs for dinner. Did you eat yet?"

He shook his head.

"Go have a seat. I need to change out of my uniform and grab a shower." She started down the hall, then paused and turned back. "Turn on the TV if you want, and there's pop in the fridge."

"Got any beer?"

She gave him a long look before shaking her head. "I don't drink anymore."

"Right. 'Cause Jesus didn't drink. I forgot. Except for that whole water into wine thing." Frank flopped onto the couch and crossed his arms over his chest.

"Frank...why are you here?"

He shooed her away. "Go change. I'll wait."

She sighed and headed to her bedroom, locking the door behind her. She stared at the flimsy knob and debated pulling something in front of the door. No. That wasn't his way. He'd wheedle. Beg, if he had to. Lie almost certainly. But he wasn't violent. Or, at least, he hadn't been. She didn't recognize him physically. It was a safe bet she wouldn't recognize his personality either.

In her old Marine Corps sweats, her hair pulled into a ponytail, Gloria went back out to the living room. Frank didn't look like he'd moved, though the news was playing on the TV.

He glanced over and his lips twitched upward. "I see you're still as girly as ever."

"It's Friday night and I just got off duty, what am I supposed to wear? It's not like I'm going anywhere. Do you want eggs, or not?"

"Yeah. You always were good at breakfast food."

She didn't bother to sigh. She could cook other things, but after a long day working, who wanted to? It had been a point of contention early on in their marriage and apparently Frank wasn't going to let the years in between temper his tongue. "Why don't you talk while I cook?"

"About what?"

"Why you're here? Let's start there." Gloria opened the fridge and took out the carton of eggs and the quart of milk. She opened the top and sniffed. Should be okay.

"Still direct, too."

"Yep." Gloria cracked eggs into a bowl. "I see you still avoid answering questions when you can."

He laughed. "I can't just stop by to see my wife?"

"You haven't had any interest in me as a person, let alone as your wife, for a number of years. Why now?"

He ran a hand through his hair. "Maybe I missed you."

The snort escaped before she could stop it. It was more likely his latest girlfriend had dumped him. Or he needed something. She beat the eggs a little more forcefully than absolutely required.

"All right, all right. I'm on my way to New York, figured this was as good a place to stop for a bit as any." He shrugged. "And maybe I was thinking I might try and convince you to come."

She shook her head and poured the eggs into a pan. "How would that work, exactly? I'm still the same person you left. If anything, Jesus is a bigger part of my life now than He was then. He's all I have."

"Then I guess it wouldn't work. I was hoping time might have convinced you to see how ridiculous you were being. I mean, come *on* Glor, it's the twenty-first century, aren't we past needing fairy tales to get through the day?"

"How's that working for you?" She grabbed toast out of the toaster and slid eggs onto two plates. "Pop or milk?"

"Is it diet?"

"No."

"Pop. I'm surprised you're not slugging down the diet. I thought that's what women did. But then, you're active."

And she didn't drink them very often. Maybe one a week. Two if she felt like living on the edge. She set a can down by his plate and took her seat. "I don't think you know me well enough anymore to comment."

Frank dipped his fork into the eggs and took a bite. "Mmm. Still got it."

Gloria bowed her head and offered a short prayer for the food and a silent plea for help before using her own fork to scrape eggs onto her bread. She folded the bread over and took a bite. "What's in New York?"

"Oh, you know. Bigger and better opportunities. No sense in sharing the details if you're not going to come along."

Which meant it was probably illegal. Certainly unethical. "How long are you here, in Arcadia Valley?"

He shrugged.

"You can't stay here."

"What do you mean? I'm your husband, of course I can."

"No, Frank, you can't. If you want to stay and work on our marriage, I'll set up counseling with the pastor." When she'd fit that in her schedule, she didn't know, but she'd do it. Even though it made her stomach clench. She pushed her mostly untouched plate away. "But until we've made some progress there...I have a friend who can probably put you up."

"Why are we still married, Gloria? I keep waiting to get papers from you." Frank scraped the last bites of egg off his plate and pointed to her food with his fork. "You going to eat that?"

"Go ahead."

"So?"

"Because it's not my call to make. We made vows before God. That means something to me. If you want to try and make this work, then we will."

He shook his head. "You take this Jesus thing to extremes, don't you? As it happens, I don't have a specific time to be in New York. I can hang here a little while. Maybe you'll come around and decide to join me when it's time to go."

That didn't seem likely. On the other hand, things were so weird now with Jonah, maybe leaving Arcadia Valley was the right choice. She sure didn't want to hang around and watch him fall in love with Kenia Akers. What was she thinking? *Forgive me, Jesus.* Sitting here across the table from her *husband*, worrying about the heartbreak of watching another man fall in love. "I'll go call Felipe."

"I still don't see why I can't stay here. I can bunk on the couch, if you insist."

"Not many people here know I'm married."

Frank started to laugh. He scooted away from the table as his mirth grew. "That's rich. I don't know much about the Bible, but I'm pretty sure there's something in there about lying being a bad thing."

"I don't lie." Not exactly. "I just don't mention it. The people who need to know, do. Felipe is one of them."

"Why not just tell people? I'm not sure I'm excited about hanging at some other guy's house. He got the hots for you?"

"Hardly. He's *happily* married. With children. And he's a cop. As for why I don't want to have you here, or tell everyone...Frank, when you leave again—*if* you leave again—I don't want to have to give up the life I built here, move somewhere else, and start over." With the kind of wreckage Frank usually left in his wake, picking up the pieces probably wouldn't be possible. "Besides. We've been separated a lot of years now. If you end up deciding you don't want to stay married to me, a divorce will be quick after all this time. You stay here, I'm pretty sure the clock resets. Do you want that?"

He sighed. "Go call your friend."

Gloria hadn't thought her heart could break anymore because of Frank, but his words—and the implied confirmation that he had every intention of leaving again and, eventually, ending the marriage—cut deep. She swallowed the lump in her throat and stood. Her cell was in the bedroom. She'd go make the call. But she wouldn't weep. Frank—and the disaster of their marriage—didn't deserve any more tears.

Gloria pulled her car into the driveway of the B&B and ground her teeth together. Felipe didn't have room. At least, that's what he said. Given how slyly he'd suggested the Fairview, she figured it was probably an attempt to push her into telling the Baxters the whole situation. She cut the engine and pushed open her door, glancing at Frank. "Let's go."

"Swank. This is a cop's house?"

She shook her head. "Nope. Another friend. She runs a B&B."

"I don't have that kind of cash. There's motel down by the highway..."

"She said she'd put you up. Favor for a friend." Of course, she hadn't given Ruth the full scoop. She needed to talk to Jonah before she did that. Didn't she? And what was she supposed to say to him? Oh, hey, by the way, that's why I've been saying no for almost three years? Gloria sighed. Tangled web indeed. Even though she wasn't *trying* to deceive anyone. All she'd wanted was a quiet life with a job she loved. And she'd had that. Then the Baxters had come to town and upset everything. She pushed the doorbell.

Ruth pulled open the front door with a curious smile. "Hi, Gloria. I'm glad you called. Most of the wedding guests left right away, so we have plenty of room. In fact, Corban and I were talking about closing for a week, taking a little pre-baby staycation of sorts."

Gloria winced and stepped into the foyer, Frank at her heels. "I'm sorry. I can find another—"

"Don't be ridiculous. One guest isn't going to be a problem." Ruth grinned and extended her hand to Frank. "Hi, I'm Ruth DeWitt."

"Frank Sinclair. Pleasure to meet you. When are you due?"

Ruth rubbed her belly, a soft smile on her face. "Not 'til April, but I feel like I'm already as big as a house."

"You look amazing." Gloria shook her head. "And when the baby comes, you're going to lose it all as quickly as it went on."

Ruth laughed. "I can only pray that's the case. Come on, I'll show you up to your room. You want to come, Gloria?"

"Is it okay if I hang here?"

"Sure. You can get comfy in the sitting room or, if you want, head back to our apartment. Corban brought me ice cream. There's plenty."

Ice cream. In January. It had to be a pregnancy thing. On the other hand, was ice cream ever a bad idea? Gloria watched as Ruth led the way up the stairs, still taking the steps quickly despite her pregnancy. When they disappeared, she followed the hall back to the apartment Ruth and Corban lived in and knocked.

"Come on in."

Gloria pushed open the door and peeked in. "Ruth said something about dessert."

Corban laughed. "Have a seat, I'll get another bowl. She goes through a half-gallon every couple of days and then complains she's putting on too much baby weight. But as far as I can tell, ice cream's about all she's eating right now."

"She must need the calcium." Hadn't she read something about pregnant women craving things their bodies needed to sustain the baby? It briefed well, at least. Given that she was unlikely to ever experience it first hand, the occasional article online when no one was looking would have to do. "I really appreciate you putting Frank up. Ruth mentioned you'd been talking about a staycation."

Corban set a generous bowl of ice cream in front of her. "It was just an idea. Helping out a friend is always more important."

Gloria poked at the chocolate scoops trying to identify the various chunks in it. Nuts, more chocolate, and were those pretzel pieces? She filled her spoon and took a bite. Definitely pretzels. Weird, but good. "How was having a houseful of celebrities?"

Corban laughed. "Honestly? Not much different from any other time we're full. They were nice. I'm pretty sure most are planning to come back for vacation down the road."

"Ruth's gifted at making people feel at home."

"She is." He smiled. "So, who's the friend?"

The door to the apartment shut with a loud click and Ruth padded to the table, lowering herself into a chair with a groan. "That was going to be my question. Brother? I don't think I knew you had a brother."

Sinclair. Of course Ruth picked up on that. Gloria cleared her throat. "He's not my brother. He's my husband."

If it had been anyone else's life, it would've been comical.

Ruth froze, her spoon half-way to her mouth, ice cream dribbling into a puddle on the table. Corban simply stared, his mouth opening and closing as he clearly searched for words.

After a long silence, Ruth dropped her spoon back into the bowl and hissed, "Husband?"

"It's a long story." Gloria pushed her bowl away and started to stand. "I should go. Thanks for—"

"Oh no. No, no, no. You sit back down and eat that ice cream while you explain." Ruth glanced at Corban before returning her gaze to Gloria. "We've got nothing else to do tonight."

Her stomach twisted into knots that would make any macramé artist proud. She took a deep breath and started at the beginning. "I joined the Marines just out of high school. We met at boot camp..."

Gloria rubbed her eyes and stared at the clock. She hadn't slept well—at all, really. Corban and Ruth had taken the news well, all things considered, but she'd left with firm instructions to tell Jonah before he found out on his own. She'd planned to do just that. Probably. It wasn't like Frank was likely to stick around once she gave him a time to show up to meet with the pastor. And that was another thing she needed to schedule sooner than later.

Four a.m. If Jonah wasn't already at the bakery, he'd be there soon.

Gloria dragged herself out of bed and into the kitchen. She needed coffee if she was going to be up this early on a rare Saturday off. The vague thought of spending the day nestled in her apartment with some sort of movie marathon had evaporated the minute Frank showed up. He had a talent for making things difficult. She winced. That wasn't fair, probably. After all, he hadn't always been that way. Deployment had changed him. And her. Unfortunately, they'd gone in opposite directions, and it didn't seem likely that he'd ever swing back the way he came. Well, neither would she. After finding Jesus, there was no going back to the kind of life she'd had before.

Where did that leave them?

Steaming mug of coffee at her elbow, Gloria flipped her Bible open to First Corinthians chapter seven. Again. She'd read the words so many times, they were printed on her brain. *If a woman has a husband who is not a believer and he is willing to live with her, she must not divorce him.* But what did Paul mean when he said "willing to live with her?" That was the sticking point. Frank had been the one to leave. Physically, he wasn't willing to live with her. But he also hadn't taken any steps toward divorcing her. Didn't that mean at some level he wanted the marriage?

Gloria sipped her coffee and closed her eyes, trying to find the words to pray, thankful yet again that the Holy Spirit knew her heart and was able to intercede for her, because she didn't know what to do beyond cry out for help and clarity.

By five, she was dressed and jogging down the steps of her building to the car. Micah and Serena would be getting back from their honeymoon later this afternoon. If she wanted to catch Jonah alone, it had to be now, before the bakery opened.

Driving through town early on a cold, January Saturday was like a trip through a winter fairy land. Ice-crusted snow sparkled in the street lights and everything was still. Frozen. Like her heart?

Gloria brushed the thought aside and lifted her hand in greeting as she passed the police cruiser idling at the corner where so many people seemed to forget to stop. She couldn't quite make out who it was behind the wheel, but at least it wasn't her. Of course, some people enjoyed the night shift, just not her.

The bakery windows glowed, warm and inviting against the darkness of the rest of the shopping center. She parked in front of the door and turned off the car. Would he let her in? She grabbed her phone out of the cup holder and dialed Jonah's cell.

Music poured into the car when Jonah answered, and he shouted over it. "Gloria? You okay?"

Her belly quivered. No. She wasn't okay. She was pretty much the opposite of that. But she had to do this. "Yeah. Hi. I'm out front. Could I come in and talk to you for a minute?"

"You're at the bakery?"

Her lips curved. "I am."

"Hang on. I'll come get the door." His phone clicked off.

Gloria stepped out of the car and hunched her shoulders against the blast of cold. She stuffed her hands deep into the pockets of her coat and moved to huddle by the door.

Jonah hurried through the front of the store, confusion evident on his face. He flipped the locks and pushed the door open. "Come on in, before you freeze. What are you doing out in this? You weren't working?"

"No. I'm off today. I...we need to talk."

His eyebrows lifted. He relocked the door and nodded toward the kitchen. "Come on back, you can talk while I work."

Of course he'd need to keep busy. He was a man down. Had been for two weeks. "How've you been managing without Micah?"

"All right. I've been doing as much as I can the night before. It's not perfect, and I wouldn't want to do it long term. In my mind, fresh baked goods need to be made same day, not prepped the night before. But so far everyone has understood. Still, I'll be glad when he's back and we can get back to normal. It wasn't nearly as bad when Mal took off. Paperwork getting behind doesn't bother me." Jonah grinned and washed his hands before returning to the mound of dough on the counter. He rolled it into a ball and began to knead, the muscles on his forearms rippling. "What's up?"

Gloria dragged her gaze away from the mesmerizing rhythm of his work and looked around the kitchen. It was the picture of what she'd term organized chaos. Dough was rising on one counter and rows of cookies were scooped on trays lined up behind muffin tins waiting, she imagined, for their turns in the oven. And the fragrance...it was always a treat to walk into the bakery during the day, but here in the kitchen while everything was being made? She'd never want to leave. Her gaze flitted back to Jonah and their eyes met. Her heart stuttered in her chest. "How was your date with Kenia last night?"

Jonah barked a short laugh and dumped the kneaded dough into a bowl before dragging a towel over the top. He went back to the sink to scrub his hands. "Did you really get up at five in the morning to ask me about my date?"

"No. Of course not. I'm just—this is hard."

"We're friends, Gloria. Tell me what's going on. It's obvious you're struggling with something."

Right. Just spit it out then. She took a deep breath. "My husband's back in town. He's staying at Ruth's. I figured I should tell you before you found out another way."

The sheet tray he'd been holding clattered to the counter. "Your husband."

She nodded.

"I see." His chest rose as he breathed in, his gaze pinning her in place. He gave a brisk nod. "I appreciate you letting me know. Don't worry about locking up behind you when you leave, Arcadia Valley's a pretty safe town."

"Jonah..."

"Don't. Just don't. You need to leave, Gloria." He continued scooping batter from a large silver bowl onto the sheet tray without looking up.

Her shoulders fell. It wasn't as if she'd expected it to go well. As quietly as she could, Gloria exited the kitchen and headed for her car. She took a last long look around the front of the bakery. It wasn't likely she'd be welcome here again. Not for a while, at least.

In her car, she lowered her head to the steering wheel and let the tears fall, her heart breaking into tiny pieces. She was married to a man she didn't love. One who didn't love her—had he ever? Really? And she was in love with a man who now despised her. As he should.

Felipe kept reminding her that the truth would set her free. He hadn't mentioned how much it would hurt.

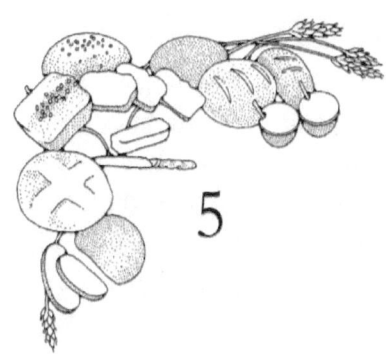

5

"Can I see you in the kitchen for a minute, Jonah?"

Jonah sighed. He'd been expecting this all day yesterday and through church this morning. Apparently having invited Kenia to their Sunday welcome home lunch for Micah and Serena wasn't going to put off the inevitable any longer. He stood and offered a smile. "I'll be right back."

"Sure. You need extra help? I can come?" Kenia started to rise.

Jonah shook his head. "I'm sure it'll be fast. Mal and Ursula should be here any minute. Would you mind getting the door for them?"

It was a flimsy excuse to keep her in the living room, but nothing else had come to him, and he sure didn't need Kenia overhearing Ruth digging for details about his conversation with Gloria.

Married.

She was married.

"What's up?" Jonah tucked his hands in his pockets and studied the efficient way Ruth handled the kitchen. She was as at home here as she was at the B&B. And she'd do just fine in a fancy restaurant, if that's what she wanted. A pang hit him and he pushed it away without much thought. He was here now. The bakery was his life. Fine dining, fancy food...that was all in the past. Well, except when he dabbled. He should have Kenia over sometime, fix her dinner. Maybe a romantic meal would bring out whatever it was that was missing from their relationship.

"You know very well what's up. What'd Gloria say? More importantly, how are you holding up?" Ruth moved a pan off the burner and set another in its place.

"I'm fine."

Ruth frowned and shook her head. "Don't give me that."

"What am I supposed to say? She's *married*. That's kind of a big deal. I would never have flirted with her if I'd known. I'd certainly never have let it go so far." He clamped his lips shut and prayed Ruth would let it go. There was nothing to be gained by sharing the fact that he was in love with Gloria. Still. Even after this bombshell. In love with a married woman. It figured.

"Hmm." Ruth shot him a knowing look. "What are you going to do about it?"

"Do? There's nothing to do. Did you miss the part where she's married? To someone else?"

"Yeah, but they've been separated for years. Didn't she tell you the whole story? Explain? It's heartbreaking."

He'd agree with heartbreaking. "I didn't ask for an explanation. Wouldn't matter. Separated is still married and, frankly, I'm surprised you'd even suggest that as an excuse. If she was divorced, fine, I could deal with that. But living together or not, the keyword you seem to be missing is *married.*"

Ruth scooped mashed potatoes into a bowl and set it on the kitchen table before crossing her arms. "You kicked her out before she could get through the whole story, didn't you? You're an idiot, Jonah."

"Married, Ruth. And I'm dating Kenia now, remember?" His gut twisted and the word girlfriend turned to dust in his mouth. She was a nice girl. Pretty and fun to be around...but she wasn't Gloria. He gave himself a mental shake. Gloria wasn't an option anymore. Nice, pretty Christian girls who were fun to be around weren't everywhere he looked in Arcadia Valley. He could make it work with Kenia. He just needed to try harder. "Did you need my help, or were you just calling me in here to beat me up?"

"Oh, Jonah." Ruth crossed the kitchen and wrapped her arms around him. "I don't mean to beat you up. I just want you to be happy."

"I know that." He gave his sister a tight hug before wiggling out of her grasp. Happy didn't look like it was on the menu though. Maybe he could find his way to content in time. "I'm working on it."

Kenia's presence at lunch had gotten a few raised eyebrows, but thankfully no one had said anything to her. Nor did anyone ask where Gloria was. It would've been a reasonable question. She was Serena's best friend and had been a big part of all their family and group activities almost since they first came to Idaho. Maybe Ruth had passed the word and asked them to keep quiet. If so, Jonah was grateful.

"So, what are you reading now?" Kenia scooted closer to Jonah on the couch, a smile playing at the corners of her lips.

Jonah cleared his throat. "I'm still working through the pile I picked up just after Christmas. With Micah out, there hasn't been any time to read during the day at the bakery. Either Mal or I have to be out front, and there's always extra baking. I'm glad he's back, if for no other reason than I can get a few pages in here and there during the day again."

Kenia chuckled. "That's a definite benefit to working in a bookstore. Plenty of reading material at hand and you're encouraged to know the stock."

"Dream job, then." He grinned and slipped his arm over her shoulder. Still nothing. It was like putting his arm around Ruth. What was wrong with him?

"You ever think of hiring extra help at the bakery?"

"I have lately. We're going to have to soon. Serena had three phone calls with her agent while they were away and there's a new script waiting for her at home. If she's away filming again, Micah's going to be heading out to see her more often."

"Do you blame him?"

"Oh, no. Not at all. But I can't handle the bakery on my own long term. Mal's hopeless in the kitchen. He can do the cashier job well enough, but he doesn't love it. Most of the folks who come in know he's deaf, but even still, people don't always remember to look his way and speak so he can read their lips. Add in that he's still self-conscious about how his voice sounds and it's not a favorite job for him." Jonah shrugged. One more thing to add to his to-do list. He should call Paige Jackson, his friend from culinary school back in D.C., and see if she had any ideas. Maybe check in with Javier Quintana, too. At least he was local and might have some local contacts. "I'm probably okay for now. At least for a little bit. What's your week look like?"

Kenia shrugged. "More of the usual. I don't have an employee just back from his honeymoon to retrain."

Jonah laughed. "Hopefully there won't be too much retraining involved. You hungry at all? I've been playing with king cakes—seems like it might be a fun thing to offer for Mardi Gras this year."

"I like cake."

"Great. I'll get us some. Coffee?"

"Sure."

He nodded as he stood. Why wasn't there a void when he wasn't touching her anymore? Sometimes he missed Gloria when he had to duck into the kitchen when she visited the bakery. It would come. It *had* to. Because

Gloria wasn't an option, which meant he either decided to be single or he made it work with someone else. Kenia might as well be that person. "Want to put on a movie?"

"Yeah. I'd like that." She smiled, her eyes sparkling.

Okay. *Please, God. Let this work. Make me feel something for her. Or make it clear what I'm supposed to do. 'Cause I'm at a loss.*

"So, how was the honeymoon?" Jonah flipped a ball of dough into a bowl and covered it.

"Why do people ask that?" Micah shook his head as he scooped batter into muffin tins. "It's embarrassing and I have no idea what to say, but it's what everyone asked at church yesterday, too."

What was wrong with the question? "You went on vacation, what's the big deal?"

"Really? *Honeymoon*, man. We weren't exactly doing a lot of sightseeing. Not outside the resort, at least."

"Oh." Heat flooded Jonah's cheeks. "That wasn't even on my radar. I'm pretty sure no one else was asking about your sex life, either."

"Yeah, well. Honeymoon." Micah slipped the trays into the oven and set the timer. "People need to use their brains and not ask stupid questions."

"Sorry. It's good to have you back, man."

"About that..."

Jonah's stomach sank. "Yeah?"

"We mentioned the script at lunch yesterday. Serena was up all night reading it, she really wants the part. She's going to fly out probably next week for a table reading, maybe the week after. But if she gets it, I'm thinking I'll want to take long weekends fairly regularly."

"That makes sense. I don't love it, but I understand it. Kenia mentioned hiring help yesterday after everyone left. I thought I'd have more time though. Guess I'll be making some phone calls this afternoon."

"What's up with Kenia?"

"What do you mean?"

Micah gave him a long, measuring look. "You know exactly what I mean. I thought she was just a plus one for the wedding. You serious about her?"

Was he? How could he be? Jonah measured flour into the bowl of the mixer to start the dough for a new batch of donuts. He hadn't been bothering with them since before the New Year. Gloria...he sighed. He wasn't going to think about Gloria.

"There's a lot going on in your brain. Does this have to do with Gloria?" Micah scrubbed at the prep counter.

"Has she been to see Serena yet?"

"I think they're grabbing lunch this week. Why?"

Jonah didn't want to be the one to tell his brother about Gloria being married. Then it would get back to Serena and that should be Gloria's to explain. Except, how long could they keep it quiet? The husband was staying with Ruth. He was pretty sure Mal knew, which meant Ursula knew. He cleared his throat. "If I tell you something, will you promise not to tell your wife?"

Micah's eyebrows shot up. "Uhh. I'm pretty sure that's against the marriage rules."

"Probably. Forget I said anything. Let's just leave it where it was. Gloria isn't an option. She made that clear and I'm working to respect her wishes. Kenia is sweet and fun to hang out with."

"So are puppies."

Jonah glared at his brother.

Micah held up his hands. "Just saying."

"I like her, okay? Maybe it's not rockets and lighting strikes when we touch, but that's not the only thing that matters in a relationship. Right?"

Micah frowned. "Don't settle, man. Maybe Gloria isn't the woman God has for you, but that doesn't mean you need to rush out and find the first available woman."

Of course it didn't. And this summer, he would've agreed that being single wasn't terrible. Except now he was rattling around in the big farmhouse by himself, all his siblings were married, and the first woman he'd loved in more than five years was married to someone else. Having someone who looked at him the way Kenia did? It filled a hole he hadn't realized was aching until it went away.

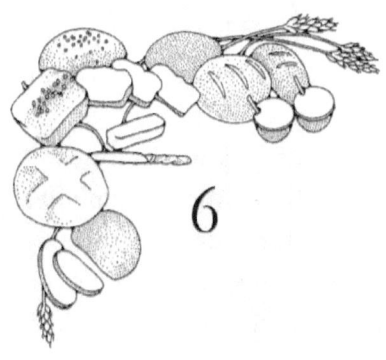

# 6

Gloria slid into a booth in the Jukebox and checked her watch. Serena was late. It wasn't too unusual, but it was still annoying. They'd put off lunch twice already this week and as much as she wanted to catch up with her friend, Gloria dreaded explaining how she was married and hadn't mentioned it to her bestie. Although at least she wouldn't be the first to break the news. There was no way the Baxters had managed to keep it quiet.

A flash of red hair at the front of the restaurant caught Gloria's eye. She raised her hand and waved.

Serena rushed to the table. "Sorry! I'm so late—I got caught up. I've got so many orders, I forgot to put things on vacation mode before the honeymoon. I sent emails explaining that it was going to take some time, but still, I need to get them handled as soon as I can. Then there's the script."

"Another one?" Gloria tucked her menu behind the napkin holder and glanced around for a server.

"It's amazing. Maybe better than the movie I just wrapped..." Serena trailed off. "You're not interested in this at all, are you?"

"Oh, no. I am." Had no one told Serena? "I guess I thought you'd have something else you'd want to talk about."

Serena frowned, clearly confused. "Such as...?"

"I can't believe Micah didn't tell you." Gloria sighed. So much for not being the one explaining everything. "Such as the fact that I'm married and my estranged husband is staying at the B&B with Ruth and Corban?"

Serena's jaw dropped.

The waitress appeared at the table, saving Gloria from whatever immediate reaction Serena had. They placed their orders, Serena never breaking eye contact.

"It's not April, so this isn't some kind of horrible joke. How did I not know this? Even if you didn't tell everyone...you know everything about me. Why would you keep this a secret?"

"It just didn't matter. I wasn't looking to date—and being a cop who's happier in sweatpants during her off hours pretty much keeps anyone from asking. Even you've pointed out how unfeminine I am. I didn't think it would ever be an issue."

"So...now it's an issue?"

Gloria turned and looked out the window, letting her gaze roam over the cars in the parking lot. Could she admit it out loud? No. There was no point. Jonah was involved with Kenia and she was much more suitable. "Frank's in town. That kind of makes it hard to keep a secret."

"Is he—are you getting back together?"

"I don't know. I've set up two appointments this week with the pastor, and Frank has blown both of them off. I'm not sure what he's doing, but he always calls and apologizes, saying he got caught up. It's so like him, I can't even drum up the energy to be upset about it. If it doesn't benefit him, Frank doesn't do it."

"And fixing your marriage doesn't benefit him?" Serena crossed her arms. "Sounds like a real winner."

Gloria winced at Serena's tone. "He wasn't always like this. In fact, if you were to ask him, he'd say it's my fault. After all, I'm the one who 'got religion.' I can't blame him, really. I'm not the same person he married. I just happen to think that's a good thing."

"You don't want him back."

"It's more complicated than that."

"How? You're not in love with him, that's obvious."

Gloria frowned. "How is it obvious?"

Serena waited while their food was delivered and said a perfunctory prayer. "Because, if you loved him you'd have told everyone about him and would be doing whatever you could to get back together with him."

Probably true. That had certainly been how she behaved at first, before Frank made it clear that it was him or Jesus. Her choice had been simple, then, and it wasn't what Frank expected. Not that he'd seemed to care all that much. By that time, he'd been drunk more often than he was sober and happily filling his hours with the women who frequented whatever bars he visited.

"I'm right, aren't I?"

Gloria nodded.

"So, if you can't fix your marriage, why haven't you divorced him?"

"I made a vow. It matters."

Serena nodded. "Okay, I can see that. But I'm not sure anyone would blame you for breaking it. Not at this point."

Gloria's shoulders slumped. "Maybe you're right."

She still didn't know what to do.

In the almost two weeks since her lunch with Serena, Gloria had kicked around her options to no avail. Frank was no help. He'd come to one counseling session with the pastor and afterward declared it a hilarious waste of time. He hadn't come back.

Ruth said he left the B&B early each morning and came back late at night. What he was doing in the off time was anyone's guess. Gloria never ran into him when she was on patrol, so he was probably off in Twin Falls or, who knew, somewhere else.

Today was it, though. She was going to figure out, one way or the other, where this marriage was going. If Frank wanted to reconcile, then he had to work at it too. And if he didn't, well, then it was time. Past time.

Heaviness settled on her chest. Divorce. It was like a big stamp of failure on her forehead. Maybe that was an antiquated viewpoint, but it was how she felt.

She pulled the cruiser to a stop in front of the Fairview B&B. It was time to get this sorted out. One way or another.

Ruth opened the front door with a pained smile, one hand rubbing circles on her baby bump. "I'm glad you called. I went upstairs to clean Frank's room. I think he's gone."

"What do you mean?" Gloria stepped into the foyer and unzipped her coat. "He's supposed to meet me and the pastor this afternoon. Not that I think he'll actually come, but..."

"Why don't you go upstairs and look, third door on the left. There's an envelope up there with your name on it." Ruth winced and drew in a sharp breath. "I'm going to make some tea. Come find me in the kitchen when you're done."

Gloria nodded and headed up the stairs. She hadn't been upstairs in the B&B before. She'd spent plenty of time in the kitchen or at the long dining room table where the Baxters gathered for family meals and parties. And they didn't limit it to family, obviously. They'd always included her, as well as Pam and Emerson and their kids, friends of Corban's since he was a child, and anyone from church who didn't have anything to do. It was the first time she'd had a group of friends that weren't part of her job—in the Corps, her friends had all been coworkers, and it was much the same on the force here in Arcadia Valley. Although, she hadn't gone out of her way to develop many deep friendships. Felipe had wormed his way in. Being happily married with kids had made it easier to let her guard down. Really, until the Baxters came to town, it was Serena and a handful of acquaintances.

Gloria opened the door to the room where Frank had stayed. It felt empty. There was nothing personal— no suitcase, no random clothes set aside, nothing that would indicate Frank was staying here. He'd never been messy. She hadn't expected to see things strewn around, but Ruth was right. Frank was gone.

Propped on the little writing table Ruth had tucked in a corner was a manila envelope with her name written in his broad scrawl across the front. She crossed the room, picked it up, and lowered herself to the straight-backed chair before opening the clasp.

A thick sheaf of papers slid into her hands, a handwritten note was paper clipped to the front.

*Gloria,*

*I think it's past time I gave you these. I've had them for several years now, but it's never seemed important enough to do anything with them. I get the dates updated frequently enough that my lawyer assures me they'll be fine as they are. Since my address of record is in Nevada, I've met the residency requirement. Once you sign and notarize these and send them in, the divorce should be final in about a week. I guess a state that specializes in drive-through weddings is somewhat obligated to have a quick solution to the problem, too.*

*I still don't think this Jesus-thing is worthwhile, but it's clearly working for you, and you shouldn't be held back from a full life because of someone like me.*

*We had some good times. That's what made me check in one last time, see if maybe you were back to the woman I remember. You'll always be a memory that makes me smile.*

*If you ever think of me, shoot up a prayer, would you? I'm not positive there really is a big guy up there, but it can't hurt, right?*

*--Frank*

Heart hammering in her chest, Gloria slid Frank's note aside, her vision blurring with tears as she read the boilerplate legalese that signaled the demise of her marriage. She wasn't sad. Not really. But it was an ending to something that had meant something to her and it probably was good that it still hurt a little. She stuffed the paperwork back into the envelope and clutched it to her chest. At least she didn't have to make the decision now.

She wiped her eyes and stood. A stack of green on the desk caught her eye. It must've been hidden by the envelope. Gloria smiled slightly and picked up the stack of twenty dollar bills, deep down, Frank was a good guy. He just needed to remember that. Maybe in time God would make His presence known. She'd keep praying to that effect.

Downstairs, Gloria peeked into the kitchen.

Ruth looked up.

"You're right. He's gone. But he did leave you this." She crossed to the kitchen table and set the money in front of Ruth. "If that doesn't cover his bill, you let me know and I'll make up the difference."

"He wasn't a guest, just a friend of a friend. I don't..."

"Keep it. Okay?"

Ruth gave a grudging nod. "Can I get you some tea?"

"I need to get back to my rounds. Are you okay?"

"I'm fine. Just tired and my head's been hurting all day, probably a pressure change. Plus, my ankles are starting to swell. All the joys of pregnancy." Ruth shrugged and sipped her tea. "What about you? You look a little pale."

"I'll be all right." Gloria studied Ruth. It wasn't just her ankles that were swollen, her face was a little puffier, too. That could be from fatigue, couldn't it? "Go put your feet up. Since Frank's gone, maybe you and Corban should close for a bit—you've been overdoing."

"Now you sound like Jonah. And Corban, for that matter. I'm all right. We've got quite a few reservations around Valentine's Day, but that's two weeks out. Maybe...maybe I'll talk to Corban about closing until then." Ruth started to stand.

"Stay put. I can see myself out. Thanks for letting Frank bunk here. I appreciate it."

"Will he be back?" Ruth's gaze caught and held hers.

"No. No, he won't."

Ruth nodded. "I'm sorry?"

"Don't be. It's time." Gloria tapped the envelope. "I'll see you later. Holler if there's anything I can do, okay?"

Back in her cruiser, Gloria set the envelope in the passenger seat and stared at it. The bank was still open. So was the church. Was the secretary a notary? It'd be worth stopping in to find out. The cashiers at the bank were all busybodies. She'd just as soon not have this news all over town before dinner.

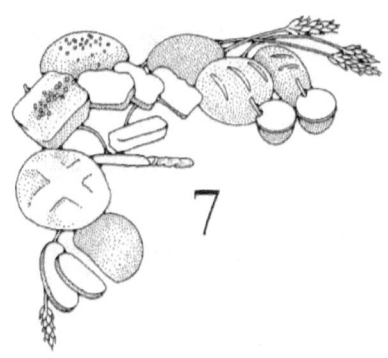

7

"No donuts today?" Kenia grinned at Jonah as she eyed the remaining treats in the display case.

He shook his head. Even though she'd decried it as a stereotype, Gloria had always been willing to sample his donuts and make suggestions for new flavors. Since she was no longer coming around, he'd lost his taste for them. "Sorry. I do have turnovers. And apple fritters."

"Ooh. An apple fritter. I'll do that." She came around the counter and wrapped her arms around his waist, squeezing gently.

Jonah returned the hug. Why couldn't it be different than hugging his sister? He needed to try harder, obviously. He pressed a kiss to her forehead. "What brings you out of the bookstore on a weekday afternoon?"

"The sun's shining, so I thought I'd stretch my legs. I can't stay long. Did you hear about the benefit concert they're putting on for Allie Bigby though?"

Jonah shook his head. "I hadn't. She lost her greenhouse and the barn where she did all her lavender stuff, right?"

"Christmas Eve. Or early Christmas morning, yeah."

"When are they holding it? I should see if we can donate some treats—maybe they can sell them as concessions for extra money."

Kenia smiled. "That's a great idea. It's Valentine's Day?"

Wow. That was going to be a quick turnaround for the organizers. Not that people in Arcadia Valley didn't manage to do amazing things when they put their minds to it. He cleared his throat. "You want to go together?"

"I was hoping you'd ask." Kenia rose to her tiptoes and smacked her lips against his. "Thanks. I should get back to the store. We're still on for tomorrow night, right?"

He nodded. Their usual Friday night date. "I'll pick you up at seven?"

"Sounds great. Bye!" She hurried through the bakery door.

Micah pushed open the kitchen door and poked his head out. "She gone?"

Jonah sighed. "Yeah. You don't like her."

"I don't not like her. She's just awfully bubbly. And talkative." Micah shrugged. "She's not really your type."

"She grows on you." Jonah paced the length of the display case. Kenia was a nice girl, but there was no spark. When was he supposed to admit that out loud? Tomorrow would be their seventh official date, and that didn't count the times he'd swung by the bookstore to say hi or they'd grabbed an hour together at the end of the day. "When did you know Serena was the woman God had for you?"

Micah's eyebrows lifted and he blew out a breath. "I...didn't realize your thoughts were leaning that way. Wow."

"No. It's not like that. It's kind of the opposite."

"What do you mean?"

"I like her. She's sweet and easy to be around, but so's Ruth, you know?"

Micah winced. "It's like dating Ruth? That's...weird."

"Tell me about it. I keep waiting for the magic to kick in and there's nothing. How long is it supposed to take?"

"I might be the wrong person to ask."

"Because it was there, right from the start. Right?"

Micah nodded.

He'd figured as much. Did it always have to be that way? Couldn't a good, happy marriage come from a friendship that slowly morphed into love?

"You should talk to Emerson."

"Corban's friend?" How was that going to help? He was another happily married person who probably didn't have any trouble navigating from the first date to the altar.

"I think he and Pam were high school sweethearts, but the three of them were friends long before that. Maybe he has insight about feelings changing." Micah shrugged. "It can't hurt."

"Yeah, maybe." There were about nine hundred ways it could hurt, and that was just off the top of his head.

"Thanks for coming." Jonah bounced his straw in the milkshake in front of him.

Emerson laughed as he slid into the booth. "Are you kidding? Any chance to get out of the house on a school night is a good one. What's up?"

"Micah thought you might be able to help."

Emerson's eyebrows lifted.

A waitress appeared at the table. "Can I get you something?"

"You know what? That milkshake looks good—cookies and cream?"

"You got it." The woman smiled and sauntered off to one of the few other tables with someone seated at it.

"I'm game to help if I can. Do I get a clue as to the topic?"

Jonah chuckled. "Yeah. Sorry. It's...awkward. I—you know I've been dating Kenia Akers?"

"Sure, Ruth's mentioned it one or two hundred times." Emerson grinned. "She's kind of excited that you're finally dating someone."

Great. "You'd think having two of us married off would be enough for her."

"She loves her brothers. So, Kenia? I don't know her, or any of the Akers, that well. Corban and I went to school with Grady, but we were a couple of years ahead of him. So I'm not sure I can give you any family insight."

"No, it's not that." Jonah cleared his throat and reached for his milkshake, then waited as the waitress dropped off Emerson's. "I've been wondering when there's supposed to be a spark. I like her. We enjoy spending time together, but it's not earthshaking."

"Ah." Emerson took a long pull on his shake. "Were you friends before you asked her out?"

"Not really."

"Would you say you are now?"

"Sure, yeah."

"Then I think I'd just give it some time."

Jonah nodded. Not exactly life-altering advice since it was basically what he'd already decided. But maybe it was good to have confirmation from someone who wasn't related. "Thanks."

"Can I ask you a question?"

"Of course."

"What happened with Gloria?"

Jonah sighed. "Nothing. She's married. There's a whole complicated story that goes along with it, but the result's the same."

"Wow. I'm sorry."

Jonah lifted a shoulder and drank more milkshake. He was done moping about it. At least in front of other people. No one had to know how many nights he spent staring at the ceiling wishing things were different. There were skyrockets with Gloria, but no possibility of anything else. Kenia, at least, wasn't already tied to another person.

"It took Pam two or three months to come around to the idea of us as a couple. I think a large part of that was her feeling that the chemistry wasn't there. I wonder if, because you and Kenia weren't already friends, you need to build that friendship first before the rest comes."

It hadn't worked that way for either of his brothers. Well, maybe Malachi, if you counted their online friendship when they didn't know who the other person was in real life. Mal and Ursula both insisted it counted—they'd known everything about each other long before they met. Sure, they'd had their own challenges to overcome, but once they'd met in person, the feelings were already there waiting to be discovered. Even Ruth and Corban had developed a friendship at the same as they fell in love. Why did he have to be different? "Thanks."

"Any time. I'm sorry if I wasn't very helpful."

"No. It's good. I'll keep on going and see where things lead. I just don't want to waste Kenia's time."

"I don't think spending time with someone who's a friend is ever a waste of time." Emerson tapped his glass. "Whether that's a quick milkshake or something more indepth."

Jonah smiled. "Good point. How're the boys?"

Emerson grinned. "Growing like weeds. Keeping me on my toes. Whoever said homeschooling was easy never had boys."

"I bet." Jonah tried to imagine spending his days teaching kids anything and shuddered. That was definitely not something in his wheelhouse. If the decision was his alone, well, wasn't that what public school was for? But Emerson made it work really well. "They're good kids."

"We think so. Pam's up for a promotion at the hospital. Neither of us are sure if that's a good thing or not."

"How would a promotion not be a good thing?"

"Pay increases are always nice, right, but it's like when I practiced law full time—longer hours, more responsibility, and suddenly you wake up one morning and realize you haven't really seen your family in over a week." Emerson shook his head. "Neither of us believe that's how God wants families to be. It's one of the reasons we moved back to Arcadia Valley. There's a slower pace here, one where you can take time to sit on the porch and enjoy the people you love. That's worth more to both of us than being the Chief of Surgery."

Chief of Surgery? Wow. "Still, that's impressive."

"She is rather amazing. I don't know how or why God arranged for the two of us to end up together, but I'm grateful. Every day."

"That's what I want."

"I hear you. It's hard to wait for it, and I say that as someone who found his wife in high school. I know that probably makes you wonder what I know about waiting, and it's a fair question, but I do understand at least a little. That said? Being on this side of things, I'd never encourage anyone to settle for less than God's perfect will."

Jonah nodded. The trouble, of course, was knowing what that will was. He'd been praying for years for God to bring him the woman He had for him. It had seemed like Gloria was that woman. In fact, he'd been more sure of that than anything in a long time. Now? It was all up in the air.

Two days until Valentine's Day. The last two weeks had slipped by in a haze of baking special orders. Apparently everyone in Arcadia Valley wanted to give their special someone a baked treat to commemorate their love. Jonah had made more heart-shaped cookies and loaves of bread than he ever wanted to do again. The last of those orders had been picked up or delivered today. They'd probably have a few more trickle in, since men weren't known for remembering Valentine's Day, regardless of the incessant advertising. But for today, he was finished, the kitchen was clean, and the ovens were off.

Jonah pulled his coat off its hook and shrugged into it. February didn't seem to be appreciably warmer than January, although Corban had already started looking toward planting so spring must be coming sooner or later. He smiled. This was his second full winter in

Idaho, and he definitely wasn't used to it quite yet. Maybe in another two or three years.

He stifled a groan. Two or three years cooking nothing but bread and sweets. Could he do it? Of course. It meant so much to his siblings. And with Ruth's first baby on the way...he'd stay. Even if every day killed off a little bit of his soul. As he walked to the car, his cell rang.

"Hey, Corban. What's up?"

"Jonah. Something's wrong with Ruth. We're on the way to the hospital in Twin Falls, her doctor said it was worth the extra time to go straight there rather than risk needing to transport."

His stomach plummeted and he fumbled for his keys. "I'm on my way."

"Can you swing by the B&B first? It's so early—she doesn't have a bag packed or anything. Just...can you get some stuff? And check the reservations? I can't remember if we have anyone coming for a Valentine's getaway or the concert."

"Of course. Don't worry about it. And if you do, we'll take care of it. You focus on Ruth. I'll be there as soon as I can. I'll let everyone know, too."

"Thanks, man. Pray. They said—they were so careful not to say anything at the doctor—but the snippets—the baby..."

"Breathe and drive. Don't borrow trouble."

"Okay. You're right. Thanks."

Jonah ended the call and blew out a breath. His heart was pounding in his chest as the list of things he needed to do scrolled through his head. He punched Micah's number as he pointed the car toward the B&B.

"Didn't I just talk to you?"

"Corban's taking Ruth to the hospital in Twin Falls."

Micah's joking tone evaporated. "What can I do?"

Jonah rattled off a few instructions, passing off getting in touch with Mal and Ursula—this wasn't something you texted. Micah could go by in person and they could come to the hospital together. He ended the call and concentrated on driving. There wasn't ice on the roads, thankfully, but the last thing he needed was to get in an accident.

Using the spare keys Ruth had given to all of the siblings, he hurried into the foyer of the B&B, and headed straight for the apartment Ruth and Corban lived in. He found a reusable grocery bag in the kitchenette and carried it into their bedroom. What would she need? He grabbed his sister's robe off the bathroom door and eyed her dresser. With a deep breath, he opened drawers and started gathering anything he thought seemed necessary. Hopefully, they'd send her right home and they could all laugh about whatever it was he had stuffed in this bag. Toothbrush. He strode back into the bathroom and grabbed toiletries.

Now the hard part. He eyed the computer. This was really more Mal's domain, but he could at least check the reservation system. They were booked solid. He opened the middle drawer of the desk and pulled out Ruth's notebook that gave sketchy directions for the system. He worked through the sequence to temporarily close online reservations so nothing new could come in. Now what? Could he and his siblings handle things for Ruth if there was a problem? They'd have to try. How did you cancel on people right before a romantic getaway? The first check-ins weren't until tomorrow afternoon. That bought them a little time.

He was forgetting something. But what? Jonah shook his head. Didn't matter. Or, if it did, it'd come to him at some point.

He should call Gloria.

His stomach jumped.

Jonah hadn't gone out of his way to interact with her since Micah's wedding. They'd exchanged a few words at church or when there was no avoiding it. But it was awkward. Still, she and Ruth were friends and it wasn't likely anyone else would remember to let her know.

He sucked in a breath and dialed.

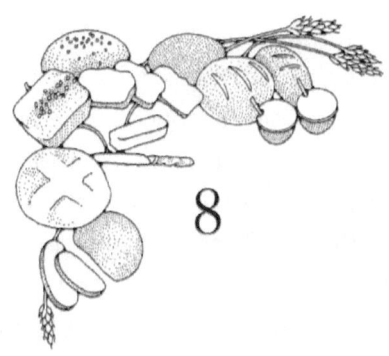

8

Gloria tore open the manila envelope and shook the papers into her hand. Her stomach clenched as the words across the top sank in. The divorce was final. She blew out a breath and tossed the papers on her kitchen table. There was nothing. Just hollowness in her chest.

It was done.

Which left her where?

The same place she'd been since she moved to Arcadia Valley. Nothing had changed, really. She was still Gloria Sinclair, former Marine, current cop. She wasn't feminine or beautiful, but she was good at her job and a loyal friend. It was enough.

She was enough.

Her phone buzzed on the table and Jonah's face filled the screen. Yeah, no. She swiped down to send the call to voicemail and turned to the fridge. There had to be something in there that would do for dinner. She couldn't face another peanut butter sandwich.

The voicemail indicator chimed. Gloria frowned. Why was he calling now? Shouldn't he be busy planning some amazing Valentine's Day date for Kenia? They were probably going to the benefit concert out at Bigby Farm, and then a late dinner at L'Aubergine. Maybe after they'd go back and snuggle on the couch at the farmhouse with some cocoa and whatever amazing treat Jonah had made.

She pushed down the fingers of jealousy that crawled up her throat. That ship had sailed. He was better off with someone like Kenia.

Gloria shut the fridge, her appetite gone, and sank to a chair. Who was she kidding?

Her phone buzzed again. Jonah. Again. Biting back a sigh, she answered, "Hello?"

"Thank goodness." Jonah's words rushed out and Gloria stilled before reaching for a pen and scribbling notes.

"I'll be right there. Why don't I grab some food—I'm assuming everyone's heading over?"

"Yeah. That's a good idea. Thanks."

"Drive safe." Gloria glanced down at her old Marine Corps sweats. They'd do. It wasn't as if she was heading to a gala somewhere. And the Baxters didn't tend to stand on ceremony. She grabbed her phone and placed a big carryout order, drawing on what she knew of the various siblings' preferences.

Halfway through the door, she stopped and turned around, rushing into her bedroom to throw on jeans and a sweater. Sweats might be comfortable, but she simply wasn't going to be around Jonah looking frumpy. She could—would—deal with her feelings for the man, but she didn't have to make it obvious to him that he was better off without her.

Gloria's thoughts whirled the whole drive to Twin Falls. Mostly she worried about Ruth, trying to force her fears into prayers. Jonah hadn't had a lot of details, but if a regular doctor's appointment turned into a suggestion to go to the hospital and, oh by the way, head on down to the one with the better NICU? That couldn't be good.

She spotted the Baxters' cars in the parking lot and pulled into a space near them. Gathering the paper shopping bags filled with takeout from the Jukebox, she strode across the blacktop, hurrying through the cold dusk. At the desk just inside the door, she paused and caught her breath before approaching the desk. "Ruth DeWitt?"

The older woman tapped at her computer and frowned. "I don't see her. You don't know the room number?"

Gloria shook her head. "She...maybe she's still in the ER."

"Sure, down that hall to the left." The woman peered at the bags. "If she has family with her, they're probably in the waiting area. They try to keep the number of people past triage to a minimum."

"Thanks." Gloria gave a tight smile and tried to keep from sprinting to the emergency room. Her sneakers squeaked on the vinyl floor as she sped through the corridor. Finally, she turned the corner and her gaze landed on Jonah, standing with his arms crossed, his face pale and blank. The rest of the Baxters were there, too. Serena sat with her head on Micah's shoulder, Ursula clasped Malachi's hand between her own.

"Hey." Gloria set the bags down on an empty chair near the group. "What have they said?"

"Nothing. Corban came out, briefly, when I texted him that we were here. He said they've got her on some kind of IV and are giving her steroid shots to help the baby's lungs develop." Jonah's voice broke on the last words.

"Lungs...but she's nowhere near term. They aren't seriously saying she's in labor?" Gloria chewed on her lower lip. She didn't know a lot about pregnancy, but giving birth in February when Ruth's due date wasn't until mid-April couldn't be good.

"Not in labor, but they're concerned about her blood pressure." Ursula patted Malachi's hand. "She's been having headaches lately but dismissed them. You know how she gets with changes in barometric pressure. Turns out maybe she should've gone to the doctor."

"So what are they going to do?" Being helpless was the worst. There had to be *something*, some kind of help.

"We don't know yet. Corban said he'd keep us posted. For now, I guess we wait." Jonah glanced at the bags of food. "Might as well eat while we do that. Thanks."

"It's the least I could do." Gloria reached into the bag and pulled out a container. She read the name of the dish scrawled across the top and handed it to Serena. "I think I knew what everyone would like."

"This is great, thanks." Serena popped open the top of her insulated container and laughed. "You know me too well."

Gloria grinned, the first easy smile since Jonah called. "You were easy. I had to guess for Mal."

Malachi took a container, opened it, and made a gagging motion.

"Sorry! Um. You can switch with me." Gloria dug into the bag, pausing when everyone started to chuckle.

Mal grinned and shook his head. "Kidding. This is fine, thank you."

By the time Corban came out again, all but his food had been consumed and the trash carried back out to the main lobby where there was a bigger can that would hold everything. Serena was dozing on Micah's shoulder and Mal and Ursula had pulled laptops out of their bags and were busy playing their game together. Gloria had tried to start up a conversation with Jonah several times, but his responses had been stilted and she'd finally lapsed into silence.

Jonah stood when he spotted Corban. "What'd they say?"

Corban shook his head. "They don't have anything conclusive, but they're finding her a bed and will admit her as soon as they have that set up. Her blood pressure isn't really coming down like it should."

Gloria frowned.

Serena yawned and sat up. "What does that mean?"

"At this point, they're calling it preeclampsia. And if they can't get things under control, they'll deliver the baby." Corban scrubbed his hands over his face. "She's only 23 weeks along. If they decide that's what has to happen, they'll probably send us to Boise by air. There's a level four NICU there. They'll know more tomorrow. The doctor said he wasn't going to wait too long to make a decision, though, because it's dangerous for both of them."

Gloria swallowed the lump in her throat. "What can we do?"

"Pray. Go home and pray. And maybe, Jonah, could you cancel the reservations at the B&B through March? I just don't see how that can work."

"I'll take care of it." Ursula rested her hand on Jonah's arm. "I know the system a little better than you most likely."

Jonah managed a wan smile. "Thanks. You're sure we can't see her?"

Corban shook his head. "I even feel like I'm in the way right now. Go home. I'll text everyone when I know more."

All the potential problems hung heavy and unsaid in the air. The baby's chances were low. Ruth's didn't seem much higher.

"Give her our love." Jonah stuffed his hands in his pockets.

Gloria watched the others stand and gather their things. Ursula and Serena both pulled Corban into long hugs while Malachi and Micah exchanged nods with him.

If the situation were different, she'd laugh at their manly attempts to show compassion without making physical contact.

Corban disappeared with his takeout container behind the double doors that separated those waiting from the treatment area and the Baxter crew began moving toward the exit.

Gloria touched Jonah's hand, ignoring the sizzle that always accompanied such an action. "Let me know if I can do anything. Anything at all."

"Thanks. I will. Though I guess there isn't likely to be anything any of us can do." Jonah stopped in the hallway. Micah, Serena, Malachi, and Ursula continued on. He cleared his throat. "Do you think you could swing by the bakery again? Even a little? We were friends, once. I'd like us to be still. I miss you."

Could she be friends with him? He was with Kenia now, would seeing him happy with someone else be something her heart could take? "I miss you, too. I can try. You're sure Kenia won't mind?"

He drew his eyebrows together, confusion written on his features. "Why would she mind?"

Gloria chuckled in spite of herself. He really didn't understand women at all. "I think it's probably worth double checking."

"Yeah, okay. But...could you come by tomorrow anyway? I was thinking of trying a new donut. You're my favorite taste tester."

She studied his face. There was a hint of something—longing?—in his eyes. No. Couldn't be. She nodded. "Sure. Usual time?"

"If that still works."

"I'll see you then. I'm glad you called me."

Jonah took her hand and squeezed it gently before dropping it. "I'm glad you came."

Smiling inside, Gloria strode out into the cold, dark parking lot. It smelled like snow. She glanced up at the clear sky full of twinkling stars. No clouds. Not yet, at least.

In her car, she plugged in her phone and started up her streaming service, punching the worship music mix that she favored when she needed to pray but couldn't find the words. She'd been singing these songs a lot lately. Tonight, at least, there was a small something to be thankful for. She'd missed Jonah's friendship. Getting that back—or at least the possibility of it—was definitely a blessing.

Hopefully, Kenia wouldn't take it away. Again.

"Hi, Mom." Gloria pulled the cruiser into a parking lot and shifted into park. She checked the time and radioed in for a five minute break. "What's up?"

"I was going to ask you the same thing. I called last night and you didn't answer."

Gloria frowned. "The phone didn't ring. You didn't leave a message?"

"It wasn't important. Where were you?"

"At the hospital with a friend."

"Ah. Hospitals always have bad signal. I think they do it on purpose."

Gloria laughed. "You're probably right."

"You sound happier than usual. You're sure you're okay? Did Frank come back?"

"No. Mom, I told you, he's divorcing me. Or, I guess I should say he divorced me. I got the final papers yesterday."

"You didn't call me? Are you okay?"

"I would've called—the thing at the hospital kind of pushed everything else out of my mind. I'm...actually fine. In some ways, I guess it's a relief."

"Uh-huh. I've been telling you to get rid of him for years, why is it okay now? At least if you'd done it, it could've been on your terms. You let him walk all over you for too many years."

She'd tried to explain it to her mom so many times, there was no point in trying again. Since her mother didn't have faith in Jesus as a starting point, trying to do things His way was a total disconnect. "Well, now it's done."

"And you're happy?"

"Happy isn't the word I'd use. I'm still sad that Frank doesn't want to get to know the Lord. I'm sad that he'd rather spend his life as far away from me as possible instead of trying to make things work and running the risk of hearing about Jesus. But I did what I could, and he ended things. So I'll let him go."

Not that it was that easy, but she'd had years of practice at this point. She'd grieved the end of her marriage for the first three years she'd lived in Arcadia Valley, even while she hung on to the hope that Frank might change his mind. At the start of the fourth year, she'd given up that slim hope and simply prayed for Frank to find Jesus, with or without her. That was, after all, more important.

"You're really sticking this Jesus thing out, aren't you?"

"Yeah, I am."

Her mother sighed loudly into the phone. "In that case, it'll probably thrill you to know that Harry has me going to church with him twice a week now."

"What? Seriously? That's great." Gloria sent up a quick prayer of thanksgiving. "How'd he swing that?"

"Seems the pastor brought his car in for service and he and Harry got to talking. Turned into a weekly thing over coffee and one thing led to another. Now Harry's pushing me to marry him, says he isn't going to keep living with me now he knows it's a sin. I figure maybe the third time's the charm, but I wanted to make sure you were okay with it. It's not like he'd be your daddy, though he's a fair sight better than that man ever was, still thought you might want to say your piece."

Gloria tried to wrap her mind around her mother's words. "I think that's wonderful. But if Harry's a believer now, I'm not sure he should marry you if you aren't one. Maybe the two of you should talk to the pastor about that."

"You really think it matters?"

"Look at my marriage, Mom. You might be okay with tagging along to church now, but if you're not going for yourself, if you're not believing because you think it's the right thing to do, then at some point it's going to become a wedge in your relationship. On the flip side, if you and Harry are both working to grow in Jesus, it's going to make your marriage stronger, too." Gloria pressed her lips together. Had she said too much?

"That...makes a kind of sense. I'm not opposed to Jesus, not like I used to be. I can certainly see the good He's done in your life. Maybe—you really think He'd be interested in someone like me?"

Gloria's eyes filled and she blinked to keep the tears from spilling over. "Yeah, Mom, I do."

"All right. I'll talk to Harry about it tonight."

"When you have a wedding date, you let me know. I'll come down to Georgia for it."

"No, hon, we're not going to make a big fuss. Probably just have the pastor do it some afternoon. You come visit when you can spend some time. Or maybe Harry and I'll throw a suitcase in the car and come on up your way. Been awhile since we took a road trip."

"Okay. Send me a picture at least."

Her mother laughed. "You can count on that. I'm sorry about you and Frank."

"Thanks, Mom. I'll be okay."

"I know that. You always are. Sometimes I worry that you're too okay. You need to let yourself dream a little."

Gloria managed a small smile, though her mother couldn't see it. Dreams were for other people. She'd learned that early on in her life and none of her experiences since then had changed her mind. She'd just keep her feet on the ground and her head out of the clouds like she always did. "Love you, Mom. I'll call you later."

9

"Dude, go back in the kitchen. She'll get here when she gets here." Micah shook his head. "You're making the pastries nervous."

Jonah's lips twitched. "Why don't you take a break? I can handle the front. You can go in the back and bug Mal."

Micah laughed. "This is just Gloria you're expecting, right?"

"I know. Sorry." He couldn't explain it. Last night, it was as if something between them shifted. He couldn't tell if it was better or worse, but his heart certainly yearned for the former. "Did you try today's donut?"

"The bacon's a nice touch. Good crunch, but not overwhelming. And I liked that there wasn't a crazy thick glaze on top like you usually find with maple bacon. This had all the flavor without the sticky sweetness." Micah pointed at the tray in the case. "They've been a big hit. Several people commented they were glad to see donuts again."

It had been nice to make them again. Jonah had never associated a particular person with a specific food item the way Gloria and donuts went together in his mind. He needed to break that, though, just in case they weren't able to stay friends. His heart panged. Even knowing it was impossible, he still wanted more than that from her. He could, at least, settle for friendship.

The bell on the door jangled and Kenia hurried in. A flash of color caught his eye and he watched Gloria park the cruiser. His stomach sank. Why did this seem like a bad idea?

"Hey, Kenia." Micah jabbed Jonah with his elbow. "Since you're here, I think I'll go see if Mal needs any help in the back."

Jonah snorted before he could stop himself. Help Mal? With what? "Hey. What brings you this way again?"

"It's okay, right? I just thought I'd take another quick break." She grinned and stood on her tiptoes to press her lips to his as the bell above the door sounded again. "Excited for the concert tomorrow?"

Jonah's gaze flitted to Gloria. What had she seen? "Oh, yeah. Of course. Should be a great time. And it'll be nice to know we're helping Allie out. Hey, Gloria."

Kenia turned and a little crease formed between her eyebrows. "Keeping the town safe?"

"One donut at a time." Gloria smiled and shook her head at Jonah. "I'll take it to go."

"You don't need to do that." Jonah slid down to the tray of bacon-topped treats and grabbed one, sliding it into a bag.

"I really do. My mom called a little bit ago and that ate up my personal time. How much?"

"On the house." Jonah fought a scowl. They were always on the house. She knew that. And she really didn't need to go. His gaze flicked over to Kenia who stood with her arms crossed, watching the whole exchange.

"Appreciate it." Gloria nodded to Kenia and stuffed a bill into the tip jar by the cashier before sauntering out, setting the bell jingling again.

Kenia shook her head. "Still?"

"What do you mean?" Jonah watched Gloria back out of the parking spot then turned to face Kenia. "Still what?"

"You're still in love with her."

"That's ridiculous. She's married. I'm dating you." Jonah's heart sped up and bile crawled up the back of his throat. The look on Kenia's face was something he'd never seen before. Well, not on her. He'd seen it plenty of times on the faces of women who were about to dump him, though. Time. They just needed time. He scrambled for something, anything, to distract her. "Do you want to try our new donut flavor?"

"You're serious? Let me ask you this, Jonah. Why'd you make donuts *today*? You haven't had any since right around New Year's." Kenia's voice was calm and had a hard edge to it that wasn't like her at all.

He cleared his throat. "Last night, Gloria mentioned she might swing by. I'd been toying with this flavor for a while..."

"Last night?"

"At the hospital?"

Kenia blinked. "You were at the hospital? Are you okay? Why didn't you call me?"

His heart sank into his shoes. He'd called everyone who came to mind when he'd been racing to get to Ruth. Kenia hadn't been on that list. Heat burned up his neck. "Not me. Ruth. She's having complications with the baby. Corban's saying they're probably getting transferred to Boise so they'll be near a level four NICU. He'll know more soon."

"I see." Kenia sighed and her eyes took on the wet shine of unshed tears. "This isn't going to work, is it?"

"Kenia. Of course it is. Some things don't happen instantaneously. It takes time." He was fumbling this. Badly. He could see it in her expression.

"I don't think we should see each other anymore."

"Don't say that." He hurried from behind the counter and reached for her hand. Kenia stepped back, her arms tightening around her waist. "Kenia, please."

"Do you love me, Jonah?"

What was he supposed to say? His heart was hammering so loudly, surely everyone within two blocks could hear it. "It's only been..."

"Close to six weeks. Are you even a little in love with me?"

"I don't think—"

"Neither do I." She took a deep breath and blinked. A tear slipped down her cheek. "Goodbye,

Jonah. Maybe...maybe it'd be better if you did your book buying online for a little bit. Okay?"

"Kenia."

She held up a hand and ran from the bakery out into the cold, clear February day. Jonah scrubbed his hands over his face. That was just perfect. Dumped the day before Valentine's Day. Story of his life.

Jonah stared at the flames that licked along the edges of the logs in the fireplace. What a completely lousy day. Just before dinner, Corban had called. Ruth had had a seizure, which threw everyone into emergency mode. They'd air lifted her to Boise and were expecting to do a c-section to deliver the baby as soon as they got there. Which meant he was probably an uncle by now.

He should be happier about that, except, of course for his sister's life being in danger and the fact that he was in love with a married woman and the woman he'd been dating was smart enough to dump him rather than keep pretending that it could work. How long would it have been before he'd had the gumption to end things with Kenia? Would he have married her? It wasn't completely out of the realm of possibility.

What was wrong with him?

Maybe it was time for another change.

Jonah glanced at the time before scrolling through the contacts on his phone and pressing send.

"Season's Bounty, how may I help you?"

"Hi. Is it possible to speak to Paige Jackson?"

"Hold on one moment, I'll see if Chef Trent is available." A string version of a popular worship song came on the line and Jonah gave himself a mental kick. Paige had gotten married about the same time he was leaving to come to Arcadia Valley. Had he ever known her new last name though?

"This is Paige." Pots and pans clattered in the background and Jonah couldn't stop the smile. The sound of a kitchen line. He missed it.

"Hi, Paige. It's Jonah Baxter. Is this a bad time?"

"Jonah? Hi. Nah, we're winding down—basically all that's left are desserts at this point. What's up?"

"I had a couple of questions. Both are probably long shots, but you're who came to mind every time I thought about it, so, I figured I'd at least start with you."

Paige laughed. "Okay. Let's have it."

"My brothers and I started a community-supported bakery in Arcadia Valley, Idaho, coming up on three years ago. We've branched out some from just breads on a subscription plan to cookies, muffins, donuts, and other bakery-type items, though our staple is bread. Anyway, Micah helps with the baking, and he's going to be in and out a lot more going forward, so we need some help. Do you know anyone into local, sustainable baking that might want to relocate?"

"Hmm. You know, I might. When would you need them?"

"Honestly? As soon as possible, but I understand packing up and moving across the country takes some time to arrange. I'd want to do an interview, maybe fly them out first."

"Sure, of course. Give me a week and I'll either have a name or two or they'll contact you."

"Perfect. The other...can you keep it sort of quiet?"

"Of course."

Jonah blew out a breath. Was he really going to do this? Not that he was doing anything. He was exploring possibilities. That didn't mean he had to follow through. It didn't hurt anyone to look. "Have you heard of any executive chef positions opening up around there lately?"

"Exec...for you?"

"There are some things here that are complicated. Seems that maybe it might be time to move. Plus, I'm not a baker. I mean, I can. And I enjoy it, mostly. But I love the line. I love creating dishes and sending them out to be enjoyed in real time. I miss that. I miss the crazy energy of a dinner service."

Paige chuckled. "I know exactly what you're saying. I haven't, but I'll keep my ears open and let you know. But Jonah?"

"Yeah?"

"Complicated isn't always bad. Make sure you're not running away from where God wants you simply because it got hard. There are a lot of things that God can use instead of a giant fish to point you back in the right direction. None of them are pleasant."

Ouch. Was he running away? Had God sent him to Arcadia Valley? Of course He had. But did that necessarily mean he was supposed to stay here for the rest of his life, miserable? "I'll keep that in mind."

"I'll be praying for you."

"Thanks." Jonah ended the call and frowned at the fire. He needed to do more praying than he'd been doing. And a whole lot more listening for an answer.

Ruth was pale against the hospital bed sheets but she managed a weak smile. "Why are you here?"

"I had to come see you and my new nephew." Jonah grinned and reached for his sister's hand. Corban had told Jonah that the doctors considered sedating and ventilating Ruth for a day or two to help lower her blood pressure, but had decided against it. That had made his blood run cold. Seeing her look as normal as she did helped. "How are you feeling?"

"I don't even know how to answer that. How are you going to get back in time for the concert tonight? And dinner? It's Valentine's Day, you have plans...you didn't cancel them just to come see me, right?"

"I would have, but, as it turns out, Kenia decided we shouldn't see each other anymore. So I happen to be free. And since I'm here, I sent Corban back to the hotel to get a few hours sleep and a shower. He doesn't look much better than you."

Ruth sighed. "Jonah."

He shook his head. He didn't want to talk about it. Not now. Probably not ever.

She closed her eyes for a minute. "Thanks. I tried to get him to do that all morning."

"He didn't want you to be alone." Jonah scooted the chair a little closer to Ruth's bed for a more comfortable angle on his arm. "When will you get to see the baby?"

"Maybe tomorrow? They say I have to be well enough to go up there. He can't come to me. Corban's been spending a lot of time in the NICU with him. You don't mind?"

"Mind what?"

"We named him Andrew, after Dad. We never really talked about it and I'd only just started thinking about it as a possibility. I thought we had all kinds of time to discuss everything."

"Nobody minds. First baby gets first choice. Corban doesn't mind?"

"No. We're using his dad's name for the middle. Andrew Nathaniel DeWitt."

"A.N.D. Cute."

Ruth chuckled, then winced. "I didn't think about his initials much. But they're not terrible."

"Are you okay?"

"Just sore. It feels like they cut me open. Oh wait, they did."

Jonah smiled. If she could joke, she really was doing okay. "Your blood pressure?"

"On its way back to normal pretty rapidly. Maybe not perfect yet, but improving. The real worry is Andrew. They started steroid shots when I went to the hospital, but he's still so tiny. He'll probably be here in the NICU until his due date." Tears shimmered in her eyes. "I don't know how we're going to manage that."

It was a very real worry. Between the money—because it wasn't like farmers and entrepreneurs had major medical insurance—and the time away from the farm just as spring planting needed to start. "We'll figure it out. You're not in this alone."

A tear slipped down Ruth's cheek. Then another and another until she was sobbing quietly.

Jonah swallowed and looked around. Should he get a nurse? "Shh."

"It's just so much."

He squeezed his sister's hand and glanced over his shoulder at the door. "Maybe I should get the nurse. Or the doctor?"

"No. Don't." Ruth sniffled and wiped her eyes. "I'm okay. I'm really glad you came."

"Me, too. I don't suppose there's any way for me to see Andrew?"

"I don't know." She swallowed and her eyes welled with tears again. "Why don't we call the nurse and ask?"

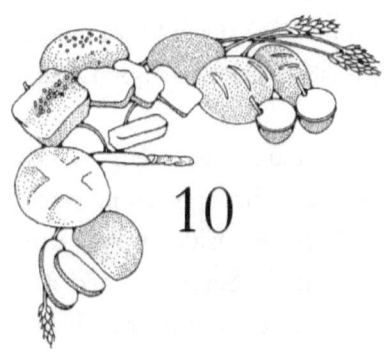

# 10

Gloria pulled her cruiser into Serena's driveway and parked. Serena's car sat in its usual spot, with another car beside it. Maybe this was a bad idea after all. She should just get back on the road, maybe swing into Demi's Delights and get a cup of coffee and something sweet for an afternoon pick-me-up, and move on. It wasn't as if she didn't have other friends.

Well. It was, actually. But she could make new ones.

Or live without.

She had the guys on the force. Felipe and Constance were definitely friends. There had to be a few others. Maybe they weren't people she hung out with on a lazy Friday night, but that could change. Couldn't it?

The door to the deck slid open and Serena stepped out. Her hair was piled on top of her head in a messy bun and she wore jeans and a ratty sweatshirt. Pottery making clothes. Gloria reached for the key still dangling in the ignition. She should definitely go.

Serena tapped on the window.

Gloria jolted. How'd she get down here so fast?

"You coming in? It's cold. I have coffee."

Gloria pushed the door open a crack. "You have company, too?"

"It's just Ursula. She went to visit Ruth in the hospital yesterday and brought some photos of Andrew. I'd planned...look, come inside and we can talk. My teeth are starting to chatter." Serena turned and hurried back up the stairs to the deck, disappearing into the house.

She could still leave. But that would be small and mean at this point. With a sigh, Gloria unhooked her seatbelt and grabbed the key. She didn't bother taking personal time. If the radio on her shoulder squawked, it'd be a good excuse to get going. And wasn't it pathetic that she was looking for reasons to leave? Maybe it wouldn't be as awkward as it seemed like it had to be.

"Hey, Gloria." Ursula grinned at her from the sofa, where she sat with her feet tucked under her. "Come see pictures of Ruth and Corban's little boy."

"I'll get your coffee." Serena stood, leaving space for Gloria to sit by Ursula.

"Hi. I don't mean to intrude." Gloria perched on the couch and took the phone Ursula offered.

Serena made a rude noise. "Please. When have I ever not been clear about whether you should stay or go? If you were intruding, you'd know. Stop being an idiot. It's gone on entirely too long."

Ursula leaned closer to Gloria and whispered, "She's still a little annoyed that she didn't know you were married. And she has crossed over into ticked that you've let things get weird between the two of you."

"I was trying to make it easier." Gloria glanced down at the photos and had to swallow. "He's so tiny."

"Just under two and a half pounds. And you made it awkward by avoiding me." Serena offered a huge, steaming mug of coffee and sat on the edge of the coffee table facing Gloria and Ursula.

Gloria sighed and swiped to the next picture. It was hard to look at Andrew, so small and yet hooked up to so many tubes and wires. She offered the phone back to Ursula. "How's Ruth?"

"Better every day. They're letting her spend most of her day with Andrew now, which I think is helping her more than anything else. She's not actually been released from the hospital, but I suspect they'll do that on Monday if things keep going like they have. Corban found a tiny furnished apartment that they can rent on a month-to-month basis so they're not commuting from here to Boise all the time."

"What about the B&B? And the farm?" Gloria frowned and sipped her coffee. Neither one of them had jobs they could do at a distance.

"I'm pitching in at the B&B. They were talking about closing down for the duration, but that just isn't feasible financially. I can still do my freelancing work—though I did let a few people know I might be slower than usual—so it works out. They have a lot of reservations starting in March, I'd hate for them to lose all of that income when I could help." Ursula stood and reached for the empty mug on the coffee table next to Serena. "Speaking of that, I should get going. I'd like to get as much done before the reservations start kicking in."

"You don't have—" Gloria snapped her mouth shut when Serena glared at her. "Sorry."

Ursula laughed. "You're in for it now. I'd feel sorry for you if I wasn't also a bit annoyed. We—the entire Baxter family—love you, Gloria. For you. Not just because we hoped you'd end up with Jonah. So get that through your head and stop being a stranger. If Jonah makes it weird, let us know, and we'll thump him. See you later, Serena."

Serena frowned. "Well. She kind of covered everything I was going to say. And she was nicer about it than I was going to be, so consider yourself lucky."

"I'm sorry. I should've told you."

"Yes, you should have." Serena smiled. "But you're still forgiven. Since your husband isn't staying at the B&B anymore, given that they cancelled all the remaining February reservations when Ruth went into the hospital, I have to ask: is he staying with you?"

Gloria took a long drink of coffee. Honesty was the better policy, always, but it was hard to trot her personal failures out, even for her best friend. She cleared her throat. "No. He gave me papers and left town at the beginning of February. The divorce was final two days before Valentine's Day."

"And you didn't...wait, that's the day Ruth went to the ER."

Gloria nodded.

"Okay. It's okay you didn't say something then. But it's been more than a week."

"I know. It's...weird. At the hospital, Jonah mentioned how he'd like us to try and still be friends. So the next day, I stopped by the bakery in the afternoon and Kenia was there shooting daggers at me. And Jonah, for that matter. I don't want to get in the way of whatever they're building between them. How am I supposed to be friends with any of you when that means I'm going to end up being around Jonah?" Gloria sighed. Honesty. Maybe Serena would have something useful to suggest. "Besides the fact that his girlfriend doesn't approve of us being friends, I'm not sure I *can* be friends with him."

"Because?"

"Because I'm in love with him."

Serena clapped her hands together and squealed. "That's so great!"

Gloria snorted. "I'm not sure which part of our conversation you missed, but there is no greatness involved in this scenario. We're doomed."

"And people say *I'm* dramatic." Serena shook her head. "Doomed is a little strong, don't you think?"

"Not really. He was in love with me when I wasn't free to love him back. Now I am—sorta—and he's in love with someone else." Gloria shrugged and finished her coffee. "Let's change the subject. Please? When do you start filming this new movie?"

Serena opened her mouth and drew in a breath. She closed it and sighed. "Fine. We can play it your way, but I want it on record that there's more to say."

"Noted."

"I don't have a firm date yet. I'll probably have to head out to L.A. sometime in the middle of March for a week or two, and maybe at that point I'll have more details."

"What's the holdup?"

Serena sighed. "The director decided he had too much on his plate and backed out. They're talking to a few others now, trying to get someone lined up but that can take time. I'm a little worried they may end up cancelling the movie. If this goes on too long, actors start to book up and scheduling gets hard. I've seen it happen too many times to count. I really want this part though."

"Ever thought of directing?"

Serena laughed. "Right."

"I don't see why not, but okay. It was just a thought." The radio on Gloria's shoulder squawked and she lifted a finger as she angled her head to listen. "I should run."

"Yeah, okay. Duty calls, I guess. Gloria?"

"What?"

"Keep in mind two things for me, would you?"

"What's that?"

"First," Serena lifted a finger, "there's no 'sorta' about your availability. You were separated for what, eight years? I don't know anyone who'd say you haven't mourned and processed the death of your marriage. Maybe you can't get married tomorrow, but it's not like you need to wait for years. Two? Kenia dumped Jonah. So he's not any less free than you are."

Gloria blinked. Jonah and Kenia weren't together anymore? Her heart began to race. That...wow. The radio buzzed again with chatter. "I have to—look, don't say anything about the divorce to anyone."

"But."

"No. Promise me."

Serena sighed. "All right. I promise. Against my better judgment."

"I'll take it." Gloria hustled down the deck stairs and jumped into her cruiser. She pushed thoughts of Jonah to the back of her mind. Now was time to focus on the job. Later—much later—she'd worry about what it might mean that they were both single at the same time.

Finally.

Gloria scooted in the back of the sanctuary as the first worship song ended. She'd spent entirely too long in the shower debating going to Arcadia Valley Community instead of Grace. But Grace Fellowship was much more her spiritual home even if she did occasionally switch it up and go to AVC, and it wasn't as if she hadn't managed to avoid Jonah for close to two months already. She could probably swing another week. Or six.

Enough. She wasn't at church to think about Jonah. She was here to worship her Savior. Except that her gaze kept straying to the row where the Baxters generally sat. It was weird not seeing Corban and Ruth there. How were they coping? It had to be hard to be so far away from home, dealing with so much. Neither one still had their parents. She and her mom didn't always understand one another, but Gloria still didn't want to try and imagine life without her.

Jonah's broad shoulders caught her eye. She dragged her gaze back to the worship band and focused her thoughts on singing.

Gloria managed to keep her attention focused on the sermon. Mostly. Maybe her thoughts—and her gaze—drifted to Jonah a few times, but that was to be expected. Wasn't it? Serena's little bomb on Friday wasn't something she was going to wrap her mind around any time soon. Technically, they could date. She'd spent so long reminding herself that it couldn't happen and now? How was she supposed to make that mental switch?

She stood with the rest of the congregation for the benediction and saw Kenia sneaking out. Gloria winced. Poor girl. Not that Gloria wanted Kenia and Jonah to be together, but still. Heartbreak was never fun.

"Come to lunch with us?"

Gloria started, her stomach twisting as she looked up into Jonah's eyes. "Um."

"Serena told me she told you Kenia dumped me. So you can't use that as an excuse. Come on, it's nothing fancy, not like Ruth makes, but I'm a decent hand in the kitchen."

She barely managed to hold back her laugh. "You're a chef. I'm guessing you're a bit more than a decent hand. You're sure?"

"We've always been friends, haven't we?"

She nodded. That was nothing more than the truth. Maybe he'd wanted more. Maybe she had, too, but even though that never materialized, friendship had been easy. Could it be enough?

"So come to lunch with friends. Everyone'll be there. Well. Not Ruth and Corban, but everyone else, so you don't need to worry about being pressured." His lips curved into a smile, but it didn't reach his eyes.

"Okay. Thanks."

He clapped her shoulder. "See you in a few."

Gloria waited for the electricity that always accompanied his touch to dissipate before she reached for her Bible and headed toward her car. A few people stopped her as she made her way through the foyer. She shook hands, smiled, and exchanged small talk. At the door, she greeted the pastor before finally slipping out.

The drive to Corban's farmhouse was short, but from the cars in the driveway, everyone had beaten her there. She stopped to rub Corban's dog Spock on the head before climbing the steps to the porch and pushing the doorbell.

Footsteps clomped across the wood floor before the door was flung open. Malachi shook his head as he pushed open the screen and pointed a finger at her. "You can just walk in. You know that."

"Sorry." Gloria signed and spoke at the same time, chuckling as Mal's eyebrows lifted.

He signed back. "Been practicing?"

She nodded. "That's about as far as I've gotten though."

He grinned. "It's more than most people know. Come on in, everyone's in the kitchen. Spock, you too. It's too cold to be out."

The dog trotted up the steps and into the house, disappearing into the living room. Gloria imagined there was a fire in the fireplace and the dog, not being stupid, was going to snag the best spot curled up in front of it. She shed her coat and hung it on the hall tree beside Serena's unmistakable emerald green wrap before following Malachi into the kitchen.

It was a cacophony. There was no other possible word to use. Jonah was banging pots and pans on the stove, filling bowls, and getting lunch on the table. Serena and Micah were already seated, talking to Ursula as she set plates and silverware around the table. Malachi dodged through the action, sweeping his wife into an embrace just this side of steamy before releasing her and dropping into the seat next to Micah. Gloria tucked her hands into the pockets of her slacks and hovered in the doorway. How had she ever believed she could walk away from this family? The last two and a half months had been miserable, and she hadn't fully realized it until she was back in the middle of the crazy, palpable love of the Baxters.

Jonah glanced over and flashed a grin. For just a moment, the noise and motion faded away and it was just the two of them in the room. A spoon clattered to the floor and broke the mood. He jerked his head toward the table. "Grab a seat, we're about ready."

"Hey, Gloria. You made it." Serena pushed away from the table and crossed the room, dragging Gloria into a hug. She whispered in her ear, "About time you were back."

Gloria smiled and patted Serena's back. "Where do I sit?"

"Here." Micah stood and switched to the short end of the table. Ursula and Malachi scooted around changing seats as well, leaving two empty chairs on the side of the table for Jonah and Gloria.

Gloria laughed. Real subtle. Obviously Serena hadn't been able to keep the news that Gloria was divorced to herself. She pulled out one of the chairs and sat.

Jonah brought the last dish, a platter with a baked chicken cut into pieces surrounded by potatoes and carrots, and set it on the table before taking the seat next to Gloria and offering her his hand. "Who's saying grace?"

"I will." Micah reached for Serena's hand and offered his other hand to Malachi on his left before bowing his head and offering a short prayer. "Gloria, why don't you grab the chicken and start us off?"

Gloria smiled and stabbed a thigh with her fork, transferring it to her plate before scooping some potatoes. "This smells amazing. What's your secret?"

Jonah snickered and reached for the platter. "I don't share that with just anyone, you know."

"He puts thyme and butter under the skin before he roasts it." Serena grabbed the bowl of biscuits in front of her with a grin. "You get the secret when you marry into the family. Or just ask Ruth. She shares them all."

"She does. It's true. And I don't even really cook." Ursula winked.

Jonah groaned. "Wow. Now I know not to share any more secrets with my sister."

"How is she?" Gloria cut into the chicken. "I keep thinking I'm going to make it over to Boise to visit and it hasn't worked out."

"She's...hanging in. They talked about putting her in a medically induced coma for the first day after the delivery to help lower her blood pressure, but she was making enough progress that they didn't."

"She's okay now, though, right?" Gloria's stomach had tightened to the point that she wasn't sure trying to eat was a good idea.

"Yeah. She and the baby both. He's a real champ. Tiny, but fighting. Corban and Ruth take turns doing kangaroo care—basically holding him on their chest, skin to skin—it's supposed to be good for both of them. But it's still hard to see with all the tubes connected to such a little baby." Micah blew out a breath. "He's going to be okay. He has to."

Gloria nodded, hearing the fierce hope in his voice. No one was going to say otherwise. If a family could make a baby thrive through sheer force of will—and probably a whole lot of prayer, knowing them—it would be the Baxters.

"Anyway. You should go see them. I know they'd appreciate it." Micah shot a look across the table at Jonah. "Maybe you two can go together sometime."

Jonah gave a slight shake of his head. "I'm going to D.C. next week, remember?"

"D.C.? Why?" Gloria's heart sped up. He wouldn't think of moving? Not with his nephew here? And all his family?

"We need help at the bakery, since Micah's going to be off hobnobbing with the rich and famous." Jonah grinned at his brother.

Serena laughed. "I keep trying to convince him it's not that exciting and that I'll come home as much as I can."

Micah snorted. "Right between telling me all the places we'll visit when you have downtime."

Serena blushed. "Anyway, the movie might not be a go."

"Aren't there people here in Arcadia Valley you could hire? Or even Twin Falls?" Gloria reached for her glass of water. "Why go to D.C. for someone? Have you even advertised the position?"

Jonah sighed. "Not yet. I was hoping to find someone whose background I knew, so I reached out to a friend from culinary school to see if she had any ideas. She chatted with her mentor from school and before I knew what was happening, things had snowballed beyond what I anticipated and now they've got eight students who'll be graduating in the spring lined up to interview with me. It's good experience for them, even if I don't end up hiring someone."

"You'd do that? Fly out there and interview but not hire? Isn't that...I don't know, it seems wrong somehow." Gloria frowned and stabbed at her food. She drove the streets of Arcadia Valley nearly every day, there were people out there who needed jobs. Maybe they didn't have culinary school under their belt, but they could be taught. Sometimes all it took was that first helping hand.

"I can't back out now." Jonah glanced across the table at his siblings. "And if Micah's going to California next month, I need someone who can start up quickly. Without a ton of training. It's...between a rock and a hard place."

Maybe. Gloria might not be a native to Idaho, but this place was her home and she wanted people to have a chance to grow and thrive here. She couldn't wrap her mind around the idea of bringing people in from outside. Although, she herself was an import. So were the Baxters. So maybe she didn't have any call to be upset. "Sorry."

"It's a valid point. I haven't advertised. Maybe I'll give the paper a call tomorrow and see what that'd cost."

"I can send an email." Malachi waved his hand to get their attention. "Kind of my job."

"Yeah?" Jonah brightened. "Cool."

"Get me a list of what you're looking for so I can work on the wording if we go ahead and place an ad."

"All right. Thanks, Mal." Jonah glanced down at his nearly empty plate. "Who's ready for dessert?"

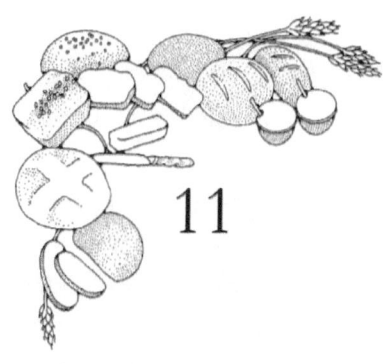

11

Jonah pulled the rental car into the parking garage and cut the engine before lowering his head to the steering wheel. He officially did not miss the D.C. area. Why had he thought he did? The drivers seemed to be intent on killing one another. Or at least making the other drivers feel like their lives were in danger. Was it some kind of contest? How had he never noticed it before?

He snagged his messenger bag and pushed open the door. It was a short walk down to Season's Bounty. The streets of Clarendon were bustling for a Tuesday night. People walked alone and in clumps on the sidewalks, dodging cars to dash across the street regardless of whether or not they were near a crosswalk.

Jonah waited at the corner until the light changed and hurried across the street. He strode down to where the wooden sign for Season's Bounty swung over the crowd, beckoning people to come eat. He pulled open the door and stepped in.

"Good evening. Table for one?" The hostess smiled from behind a small wooden podium.

"Actually, I'm Jonah Baxter. I think Paige is expecting me?"

"Of course. If you'll follow me, I'll take you through to the kitchen."

Jonah trailed behind the hostess, taking in the layout of the main dining area. It was a good space, well utilized. He'd probably tweak a few things, if it was his, but it was clear Paige knew what she was doing. Whatever had moved her from catering to this restaurant had ended up being a good decision.

Stepping into the kitchen was like entering another world. The sounds of pots and pans clanged together. Cooks shouted to one another as they plated food and sent it down the line to be delivered to the customers out front.

"Jonah!" Paige adjusted a plate before handing it to a waiting server. "Come on back to the office. There's a bundle of nerves waiting for you."

He could imagine. "Part of the job, right?"

"Yeah. Still, go easy on 'em if you can. They seem like good kids. Do you mind if I sit in? I was thinking we could always use a little part time help, and I like to give back when I can."

That made it a little better. Gloria's words from Sunday still lingered in his brain. Was he doing the wrong thing by looking to hire from out of town? He'd almost canceled his flight, but he couldn't justify losing that kind of money. So here he was. If nothing else, he'd get a chance to practice his interviewing skills.

A little distance from Gloria wasn't bad, either.

Jonah pushed that thought away. Just because she was married didn't mean they couldn't be friends. Especially now that Kenia was out of the picture. He sighed. That ought to sting more than it did. Another thing to worry about later.

Paige wasn't kidding about the bundle of nerves. Four kids—he couldn't call them anything else—sat on chairs in the short hall off the office. All of them were palpably nervous. He lifted a hand and smiled. "Evening. Thanks so much for taking time out to come and chat with me."

"Why don't we just go in the order you're sitting." Paige pointed to the girl twisting her fingers together in her lap. "Lindsay, right? Come on in."

Jonah slid along the wall of the tiny office. How had Paige wedged three chairs in here? He sat and glanced at Paige.

Paige shook her head. "You go ahead. I'm just hanging out."

Great. He smiled at the young woman and cleared his throat. "Okay. Why don't you tell me a little about yourself?"

"I still don't understand why you're in D.C. to interview people. There have to be potential employees in Idaho." Exhaustion and strain were evident in Ruth's voice even over the phone line.

Jonah licked his lips. "I—I was also thinking of looking for another chef position."

"We don't need a chef."

"No. For myself. Out here." Jonah frowned at the window of the hotel room. Even with two sets of thick curtains and whatever else hotels did to try and guarantee a good night's sleep, traffic noise wormed its way into the room.

"But—no. You can't do that. Why would you do that? Now more than ever we need you, Jonah." Ruth's voice hitched.

Great. He'd made his sister cry. It wasn't hard to do right now, but still. How was he supposed to explain? "I miss cooking stuff that isn't bread. I never wanted to become a pastry chef, either. And yet now I spend all my time doing exactly that. When I get home, I'm too tired to bother with something more interesting than a PB&J, so I can't even cook on my own time."

"So? There are restaurants in Arcadia Valley. And Twin Falls. I'm sure there's someone who'd hire you part time. Or, I know, add a café on to the bakery. The kitchen would handle it. You're finished with the baking by mid-morning, you could at least open for dinner. Maybe even lunch."

Soups and sandwiches. Café didn't exactly scream real cooking. Would it be enough? Even if it fixed the yearning to do more than knead dough and scoop out muffins, it didn't address the real problem. "And then there's Gloria."

Ruth's sigh crackled over the phone. "I was hoping the two of you were back to friends. Micah said she was over after church."

"She was. We are. I guess. It's hard." He couldn't quite bring himself to get into the details. Jonah was fairly certain he was in love with Gloria. Still. What did it say about him that he could be in love with someone who was married to another? That he wanted to plead with her to leave the guy? How could he live with himself if he convinced her to do that? How could he stay in Arcadia Valley if he didn't? That one was easy to answer. And it was one reason he was back in D.C. He could enjoy it here again, couldn't he?

"All of life is hard. You think a micro preemie isn't hard? God doesn't promise us easy. He only promises to walk beside us. Sometimes, He does that in the form of our family. I need you here. We all do."

"I'll be home on Thursday."

"For how long?"

He didn't have an answer. "I love you. You know that, right?"

"Yeah I do. I love you, too. Come home, Jonah. Don't run away."

"I should get to bed. Take care. Kiss my nephew for me." Jonah ended the call and stared up at the ceiling. He wasn't running away.

Was he?

He paused for a moment and stretched his back, his spine emitting a couple of satisfying cracks as the vertebrae settled back into place. "Time on the filet?"

"Need two minutes." The chef on the meat station pressed his finger into the beef in question and nodded.

Jonah gave a practiced flick with his wrist and sent the vegetables in his sauté pan into the air, catching them before giving another firm shake to the pan. With a light touch, he sprinkled seasoning and checked the other sides that would accompany the filet. With another minute left, he began plating, leaving room for the most important element of the dish.

"Filet." The chef slid a plate holding the meat down to Jonah.

Jonah checked the doneness and carefully arranged it on the plate before walking it to the window. The other orders for the table were on their way to the window as well. The head chef eyed the plates, tweaked a few items, and rang the bell for pickup.

"Nice job, Baxter. You're really thinking about relocating?"

Jonah nodded with more confidence than he felt. He was thinking about it. After his conversation with Ruth last night, he wasn't as sure it was the right move as he had been, but the thought was still there.

"You've got a job here if you want it. I need a reliable second-in-command. It's clear to me you haven't lost any of your skill even after three years slapping bread dough around."

Jonah grinned, but his heart sank. This was what he'd been hoping for. Why wasn't he reaching for a handshake and arranging a start date? "Can I get back to you?"

"Sure. We're getting along okay, but when I heard you were interested in coming back to town, I knew I wanted to scoop you up."

Jonah managed a weak smile. This was exactly what he wanted, and yet all he could hear in his head was Ruth asking why he'd leave right when they needed him most. And Gloria...thoughts of her pushed him away almost as much as they rooted him in Idaho.

"We're winding down. If you want to go get cleaned up, I'll join you out at the bar in about twenty. We can talk details."

"Great. Thanks." Jonah slid behind the guys prepping the last dishes of the night and turned into the small staff room. It was essentially a closet with a few lockers jammed into it so people had a place to store their personal items. He shrugged out of the borrowed chef's jacket and tossed it at the hamper in the corner of the room.

Out on the restaurant floor, he skirted the edge of the room, avoiding the diners who were lingering over a late meal or dessert, and found an empty stool at the bar. After catching the bartender's eye, he ordered a ginger ale and pulled a bowl of peanuts closer. He wasn't hungry, but it was something to pass the time.

His phone buzzed with a text and he slipped it from his pocket. Gloria. His heart sped up.

*Ruth said you'd be home tomorrow?*

Jonah tapped back an affirmative.

*Any luck with hiring?*

He frowned and hit call. Why text when he could get a chance to hear her voice? Even as he tried to push those thoughts away, she picked up.

"Hey. I didn't want to interrupt."

"It's all good. I'm just waiting for a friend. To answer your question, no. The candidates were all solid, but no one felt like a great fit. I guess I should text Mal and let him know he should go ahead and run that ad."

Gloria chuckled. "He might have already started it."

Of course he had. Jonah shook his head. "Any takers?"

"That I'm not privy to. I just happened to be checking in with Serena when Micah mentioned something."

"I guess I should call my brother and check in." Jonah smiled. Knowing Mal and Micah, they probably had interviews lined up for next week. "Other than that, how's Arcadia Valley?"

"Pretty much the same. We set up a speed trap over by the high school. Taught quite a few seniors a lesson about school zone safety."

"Ouch."

"Wasn't my idea. I kind of agree with you. On the other hand, those limits are there for a reason. The bakery looked like it was doing okay without you, although Micah shouldn't try to make donuts."

"Why not?"

"They were soggy. And yet somehow still kind of burnt tasting."

Jonah smothered a laugh. How had he managed that? It wasn't like they were frying the things. Baked donuts were next to foolproof. "I'll try and give him some pointers when I get back. Everything else taste okay?"

"You think I sample everything in the case? After that donut yesterday, I didn't even stop in today. It's…not the same without you there."

Jonah's heart swelled. Of course she meant the food. Not him. She was as off limits as they came. But it was still nice to be missed. "Yeah, well, D.C. isn't quite how I remember it, either. It's—"

"Hey. Oh, sorry." Jonah's friend slid onto the stool next to him and signaled the bartender.

"I have to run. I'll be back tomorrow. So Friday, the baked goods should be back to normal."

"I'll try to stop by. Be safe. A lot of us miss you."

Jonah hit end and tucked the phone back in his pocket. "Sorry about that."

"No problem. Girlfriend?"

Jonah hesitated then shook his head. "Just a friend."

"Uh huh." He drummed his fingers on the bar top. "All right, let's talk details."

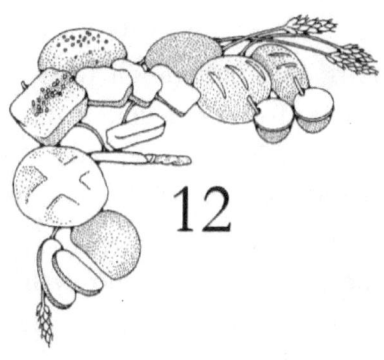

# 12

Gloria parked in front of A Slice of Heaven and cut the engine of the police cruiser. She pushed open the door and drew in a deep breath. Spring was definitely in the air. She could smell hints of it on the mid-March breeze.

The bells above the door jingled happily as she stepped through.

Jonah looked up from his book and stood, his lips curving into a smile. "Hey. Back again?"

She willed her heart to slow down. It had been a month—to the day—since her divorce, and she and Jonah had returned to their even footing as friends. It could be enough. It would have to be. She'd had her chance with him, now that he knew she'd been married he couldn't possibly be interested. "You know me. I can't seem to help myself."

He laughed. "I count on it. Especially with Micah out of town this week, I don't have anyone to try my new creations."

"Mal won't sacrifice for the cause?" Gloria crossed to the coffee pot and filled a mug with the rich blend of coffee Grant Ward made for the Baxters. She stopped by nearly every afternoon for a whole host of reasons, and the coffee was definitely one of them. She splashed in a hint of half-and-half and a packet of raw sugar before settling at one of their small tables. "That seems unsporting of him."

"Oh, he tries them, but mostly he just says it's good. No explanation. When I push, he doesn't have anything more to add but a shrug."

She could see that. "All right. What's today's creation?"

"Hang tight, let me run in the back and grab it. I wasn't sure enough about this one to do more than a small batch for some taste testing."

Gloria sipped her coffee.

Jonah was back quickly with a plate holding two donuts. He set it down in front of her and took a seat, nodding toward the snack. "Go ahead."

It looked like a regular chocolate glazed donut. Except a little lumpy on top. Gloria poked one of the lumps. Springy. She picked up the pastry and bit into it, her eyes widening as she chewed. "S'mores?"

He nodded. "Do you get the graham cracker at all? I wasn't sure there was enough."

"It could use a little more, but it's good. The marshmallows are what threw me. There's no toasted taste, but I'm not sure how you'd manage that."

"Yeah, it's tricky. I'll have to play with them a little more. Do you want something else?"

"No, this is fine. Thanks." Gloria glanced over at the display case and reached for some topic of conversation. They still had these little lulls, where normally there would've been some banter, something that tiptoed on the edge of flirting. That was gone. Would it ever come back? "I saw Corban out in the fields this morning. How are they doing?"

"About as well as can be expected, I guess. Ruth's still in Boise in their apartment. She spends her days with Andrew. Her blood pressure is back to normal, but she'll have to keep an eye on it for a while yet. They're thinking they can all come home right around his due date, so maybe another month? I'm not sure what milestones they're looking for beyond breathing and weight gain, but I think there are a handful of others."

She couldn't imagine. Of course, having been there close to two months, being within a month of coming home had to feel good to Ruth and Corban. "I'll try to get out there again to say hi. Maybe...maybe on my next day off we could drive over together?"

Jonah glanced toward the kitchen door.

"Or not. That's fine, too." Gloria offered a weak smile and shoved the rest of the donut into her mouth. It was time to get going. Trying not to choke while she chewed, she swigged her coffee to wash down the treat. When her mouth was empty enough to speak, she cleared her throat. "I should get going."

"I...you don't have to go."

"I really do. Thanks for the donut and coffee. Can I pay you?"

He frowned. "No. Gloria, you know better than that."

Did she? But now wasn't the time to dig into it. It was very possibly never going to be the right moment for that particular conversation. No matter how much she thought she wanted the answers. She was also half-convinced she absolutely *didn't*. Gloria pulled her wallet out of her pocket and fumbled for a ten. "You can't feed me for free every day. Here. Take it. Put it in tips if that's what you want to do."

Jonah didn't move as she stuffed the money into his hand.

"I'll see you later." Gloria swallowed the lump in her throat and rushed out the door. Had the last month been a colossal misunderstanding? Were they not back to being friends? She yanked open the cruiser's door and threw herself behind the wheel. She'd prayed that maybe, now that they both were free, she and Jonah could find their way to one another. A single hot tear slipped down her cheek as she backed out of the parking spot. Clearly she was wrong.

Gloria headed down Main, aiming for the high school. She was in the mood to write some tickets.

"I'm sorry. That sounds awkward." Felipe pulled the lever on the recliner, lifting his sock-clad feet. "Are you sure he knows?"

"He has to." Gloria twisted her fingers together in her lap. "Serena's awful with secrets. And I'm sure she told Micah. Even if she said she wouldn't. What brother is going to keep that quiet?"

"One whose wife asked him to?"

Gloria frowned.

"It is a possibility. Right?" Felipe dipped into the bowl of nuts that sat on the arm of his chair and jerked his chin at the plate of food next to Gloria on the couch. "You should eat something before Constance gets back in here or she'll be mad. You don't want that. Trust me."

Shaking her head, Gloria picked up a triangle of quesadilla and took a bite. Was it possible Jonah didn't know she was divorced? "So, what? If he doesn't know, what do I do?"

"Tell him?"

Gloria snorted.

"What? Men don't read minds, Gloria. I've never understood women who think we're supposed to. I wouldn't have pegged you as one of those types either."

"It's true. They don't." Constance bustled in from the kitchen and sat with a sigh. "I keep hoping he'll develop the skill, but so far no dice. Who's supposed to read your mind?"

"Jonah Baxter."

"The baker? It's about time." Constance gave Gloria a speculative look. "He's handsome. Not a mind reader, of course, but worth a second look."

"Should I be worried?" Felipe grinned at his wife.

"Oh, please. He's much too young for me. But just about right for you. I'd say go for it."

Gloria chuckled. Constance could always lift her spirits, almost as easily as Felipe. "Just like that?"

"Why not? It's the twenty-first century, you don't have to wait around for a man to notice you anymore. You're a smart, capable woman. If you've prayed about it, and you feel like God's saying go ahead, then why wait?" Constance shrugged and pointed to the plate of food. "And eat. You're too skinny."

Felipe sent Gloria a look that practically screamed 'I told you so.' "He's already noticed her."

Gloria reached for another triangle of tortilla and melted cheese.

"So what's the problem?" Constance angled her head at Gloria.

"He might not know I'm available." That was easier than going over the whole story again. Felipe could fill his wife in later, if he wanted.

"So tell him." Constance shook her head. "Honestly, sometimes young people make it all seem so hard. Have a conversation. Be honest."

Gloria couldn't stop her smile. "You're not exactly old, you know. You two have what, fifteen years on me?"

Felipe laughed. "Closer to twenty. But still, you notice we gave you the same advice. Pray. Then go talk to the man."

Gloria hunched her shoulders. Could she go back and talk to him after the fiasco this afternoon? She'd planned to steer clear of the bakery for a few days, give them both time to find their footing again. Sunday would be here soon enough and maybe by then she wouldn't want to sink through the floor at the thought of making eye contact. Praying about it some more was definitely the first order of business. "Yeah, okay."

"You wanted a different answer."

"I don't know what I wanted." Gloria chewed on her lip. "Actually, I do. Three months ago, I couldn't get the guy to stop asking me out. Now he wouldn't even agree to go visit his sister and nephew in the hospital with me as friends. Knowing what I do now, I never should've told Jonah—or anyone—that I was married."

"So you planned to hide that marriage for the rest of your life?" Felipe shook his head. "Secrets never work out the way you want them to."

"Not forever. But maybe I could've just mentioned it, casually, after we'd been dating for a while and everything was secure."

Constance reached over and patted Gloria's leg. "You have to know that would still have caused problems."

"Yeah. I guess."

"Love can be hard." Constance smiled. "Sometimes I think that's what makes it worthwhile. I made brownies this afternoon. You want one?"

Felipe raised his hand. "I do."

"No. I should get going. Thanks, Felipe. Constance. I appreciate the two of you. Even when you don't tell me what I want to hear." Gloria stood and grabbed the plate off the couch.

Constance tugged it gently from her hands. "I've got this. Keep us posted. We'll be praying for you."

Gloria nodded. If she were a hugger, she'd give her friend and his wife a long, hard squeeze. She'd had the briefest flicker of an impulse to do just that, but she tucked her hands in her pockets instead. "Good night."

The drive to Boise had given Gloria plenty of time to think and pray. She'd tried to call Serena on Thursday night after she got home from Felipe's, but the call had gone to voicemail. She hadn't wanted to leave a message effectively accusing her best friend of breaking her confidence, so she'd hung up after just saying hello and asking how the meetings were going. More than likely, Serena would know something was up. It wasn't like Gloria to call while Serena was out of town. But it was the best she'd been able to do.

She parked in the hospital's garage and wound her way through the corridors to the NICU and pressed the intercom button outside the locked doors.

"Can I help you?"

"I'm here to visit Ruth DeWitt? I'm her friend, Gloria."

"I'll go let her know. You can have a seat in the waiting room there on the left."

Gloria glanced over and noticed the little room for the first time. No one sat in any of the faux-leather chairs that lined the walls. Magazines were scattered around on the seats. She sat and pulled out her phone. If Ruth were busy with the baby, it might be more than a couple of minutes. The last thing she wanted to do was pull her friend away from Andrew if he needed her.

Her phone chimed. Gloria tapped the text icon and grinned as a photo of her mother dressed in a baptismal robe standing with a man in a pool of water filled the screen. The next photo showed her mom emerging from the pool grinning.

She tapped out a reply. *"Wish I could've been there. Congratulations! I'm so happy for you."*

*"I thought about waiting until you could be, but Harry was so excited when I accepted Jesus, that I wanted to do this right away. We'll probably get married next week."*

Next week? There was no possible way Gloria'd be able to swing vacation that fast. Of course, her mom didn't really need her there. Harry was a good guy. Maybe now, since they were both following Jesus, things would work out better. Not that Christians didn't get divorced. She was living proof of that. As were plenty of couples where both members professed Christ. Still, shared faith and a determination to live for Him had to help.

*"Sorry I'll miss it. Congrats to you and Harry. Come visit when you can."*

Gloria looked at the photos of her mom's baptism again and smiled, offering a quick prayer of thanksgiving. She'd been praying for her mom for so many years, it was good to see that some prayers were answered in the affirmative. Maybe, just maybe, her prayers for Jonah would be as well.

"Hey." Ruth shuffled into the little waiting area. "I wasn't expecting you today."

Gloria stood and let Ruth wrap her arms around her. She patted Ruth awkwardly on the back before stepping away. "I did text. Is it okay? I wanted to see how you were doing."

"You texted?" Ruth frowned and pulled out her phone. "So you did. Sorry, I don't know how I missed that. Sometimes my notifications get weird. Of course it's okay. I appreciate you making the drive. You want to go down to the cafeteria? I don't like to be gone long, but a lunch break is never a bad idea."

"Sure."

"Then, if you want, you can come in and see Andrew. Corban isn't going to be back until later this afternoon, so we'll be under the two-person limit."

Gloria smiled. "I'd like that."

Ruth asked about the happenings around town as they strolled through the halls and rode the elevator down to the cafeteria. It was clear she made the trip regularly, since she barely had to pause at any of the intersections. Gloria was pleased to have the majority of the answers, although she hadn't checked in with Ursula and didn't have the most up-to-date scoop on the B&B.

"Don't worry about it. I'll give her a call tonight. I can still log in to the reservation system from here. Corban rigged up my laptop so I wouldn't go crazy wondering. I know we have two couples staying for a week, but I miss getting a chance to meet them and find out the little tidbits people let drop when chatting with a nosy innkeeper."

"Friendly." Gloria grabbed a tray from the stack and handed it to Ruth before taking one for herself. "I don't think you're nosy. Although..."

Ruth laughed and set down her tray before sliding some to make room for Gloria. "That's quite a lead in."

Heat spread over Gloria's cheeks. She probably could've been a bit more subtle. But since it was one of the reasons she'd made the trip today, she hadn't wanted to forget to ask. "Sorry. I—do you remember the day I came over and Frank had already checked out?"

"Of course. You looked so upset when you left, but you didn't want to talk about it." Ruth reached for a salad.

Gloria slid past the salads and pointed to the hamburgers. The cafeteria worker slapped a burger onto a bun. He pointed to fries and she nodded. She still didn't really want to talk about it, but she needed to know. "Do you remember the envelope he left for me?"

"Sure."

"Did you look in it before I got there?"

Ruth turned and crossed her arms. "Seriously? So you do think I'm nosy."

"No. I—" Gloria sighed. "I'm sorry. Don't be mad, please."

Ruth grabbed a bowl of gelatin from the last case and headed toward the cashier.

Gloria reached for cake and hurried after her friend. "Let me get it."

"If that's what you want."

She'd really made a mess out of this. Maybe—hopefully—Ruth would give her a chance to explain. Gloria followed Ruth to a small table by a window that looked out over the parking lot. "Nice view."

Ruth's lips twitched. "It's better than the other side of the cafeteria. That looks out over the dumpsters."

"Parking lot it is." Gloria pulled out her chair and sat. She offered a brief prayer over her food and glanced at her friend. "Can I explain?"

Ruth nodded and dumped dressing all over her salad.

Gloria blew out a breath. "So, the envelope? It had divorce papers in it."

Ruth's eyebrows shot up. "Whoa."

"Yeah. I'm guessing that's why he was in town in the first place, to make sure I got them. Why he didn't just drop them and run, I don't know. But it's good, I guess, that he didn't. It helped me see, for certain, that he was never going to accept me as long as I love Jesus. I mean, I knew it. I've known it for years. But there really was nothing I was ever going to do that would change his mind."

"Of course not." Ruth frowned.

"I know you probably think I'm an idiot for not divorcing him myself a long time ago. You're not alone. I had good reasons—or I thought they were good.

Anyway, I signed them. I got the final decree two days before Valentine's Day."

"Oh. That was the day..."

Gloria nodded.

"So did you tell anyone?"

"Not until later. I mentioned it to Serena, but asked her not to tell anyone. It looked like things with Jonah and Kenia were going so well, I didn't want to muddy the waters."

Ruth snorted. "She dumped him. The day before Valentine's Day. She realized he was in love with you, even if he's never been willing to admit it to anyone out loud."

Gloria blinked. Ruth was so matter of fact. Sure, her heart thrilled to hear it. Even if Ruth's information was out of date, there had been a time when he'd loved her. Was it possible they could work their way back to it? "Are you sure about that?"

"Oh, yeah. I know my brothers. He hasn't asked you out? Now that you're free?"

"I—he doesn't know. I guess. If you didn't know, and Serena didn't say anything to Micah. I haven't told him." Gloria pushed her untouched food away from her. There was no point in trying to force food into her system. Her stomach was clenched so tight, she wasn't sure swallowing would do more than get something stuck in her throat.

"What? Why not? Or do you not like him after all?"

"I do. I...I'm in love with him. I have been for probably a year, even though it made me hate myself."

"Ooh. I can see that. But now?"

"I've been swinging by the bakery again in the afternoons. We chat and have fun—it's almost the same as it was before. There are a few awkward pauses. So I asked if he wanted to come down and see you with me. I thought—hoped—maybe a day trip together would get things moving. I was sure he knew about the divorce, though. So when he said no—I figured maybe he'd changed his mind."

Ruth closed her eyes. "I swear the two of you are going to drive me to an early grave. Just talk to him. Tell him. Even if he does know—which I don't think is the case—he's going to need to hear it from you."

"Okay. I...thanks."

Ruth glanced over at Gloria's plate. "Are you going to eat?"

Gloria shook her head.

"Let's head upstairs then. You can hold the baby." Ruth grinned. "That always makes me feel better."

Gloria stood and reached for her tray. She wasn't positive holding a tiny baby was going to do anything other than stir up feelings she wasn't ready to deal with, but spending a little more time in Ruth's soothing presence was what her soul needed.

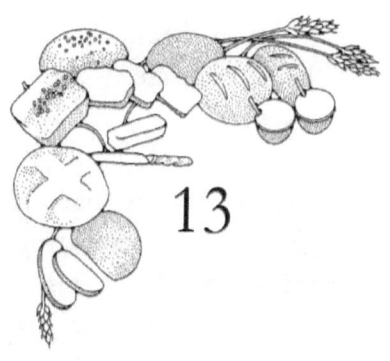

# 13

Jonah paced the length of the kitchen. He hadn't been to church in two weeks. Skipping seemed easier than working to avoid Gloria. With Ruth and Corban in Boise and Micah and Serena in L.A., bailing out of hosting a family lunch had been easy enough. He'd heard from Corban that Gloria had been to visit Ruth. His heart panged. He could've gone with her. Seen Ruth and his nephew.

Spent the day with Gloria.

And that was the problem. He wanted that. Too much. She belonged to someone else.

His hands clenched into fists.

Oh, sure, Frank had seemed like a nice enough guy. But if she wanted him, why hadn't she gone with him when he left? Why didn't he stay? How could Frank be married to someone as amazing as Gloria and not appreciate it?

She'd been coming by the bakery, off and on. He'd made Malachi man the front and spent his time hovering by the kitchen door. She'd asked after him. The first couple of times, Mal had come back and tried to get Jonah to come say hi. He'd pleaded work.

He ached to see her.

*She's not free.*

He wasn't big on tattoos, but maybe that was something he ought to consider having permanently inked on his arm as a reminder to his wayward heart. Or...his friend in D.C. had called again last night. Maybe leaving was the better course of action. For everyone concerned.

Malachi slammed through the swinging door that separated the kitchen from the front of the bakery and started signing furiously.

"Whoa. Slow down." Jonah held up a hand and tried to focus on his brother's wildly moving hands.

Malachi stomped his foot and started over. When he was finished, he pointed at the door and raised his eyebrows.

Jonah swallowed. Gloria was here and apparently his brother was done running interference for him. "Fine."

Gloria looked up as Jonah entered, a hesitant smile on her lips. "Hi. I don't think I've ever seen Malachi that angry."

Jonah tucked his hands in his pockets and hovered behind the cash register. "It doesn't happen often. But he can be a force to be reckoned with when he wants to. What can I get you?"

"I just wanted to say hi. I feel like you've been avoiding me. And...I have some things I'd like to say."

"So do I."

"Okay. Um. Do you want to go first?"

He nodded, his heart hammering in his chest. "Micah should be back tonight. I've got a couple of high school students coming in before and after school to help with the baking. They're working out well enough. As long as someone's here to keep them focused and on point. Micah and Malachi are both capable of that. So. I'm taking a job in D.C."

Gloria's lips parted and she drew in a sharp breath. She clamped her mouth shut and glanced to the side. "Wow. No wonder Mal's mad. I...you'll be missed."

Were those tears in her eyes? Jonah fought the urge to leave the safety of the counter that separated them and pull her into his arms. That way led to madness. Even if she'd been going to say she'd miss him. It could only be as a friend. "I'm sure I'll be back to visit. My whole family's here. What did you want to say?"

"I'm not sure it's relevant anymore. I'll let you get back to work. I'm sure there must be a hundred things you need to do before you go. When do you start?"

A hundred and one if he counted actually telling his friend in D.C. he was taking the job. "We haven't firmed those details up yet. Why don't you let me decide if it's relevant or not?"

Gloria hesitated, one hand on the door. Finally she gave a small nod. "Frank divorced me. It was final on Valentine's Day."

Jonah's breath caught in his lungs and a thousand thoughts all clamored for priority in his brain. By the time he'd gotten a handle on the racing chaos, Gloria was backing out of her parking spot. Should he run after her? And tell her what? How much did this really change?

"If this is an April Fool's joke, you need to have your sense of humor recalibrated." Micah stomped into the living room of the farmhouse and stood in front of Jonah's recliner, hands on his hips.

Jonah took the time to slip his bookmark between the pages of his latest read—ordered online, because he wasn't sure just how long he was supposed to stay away from Page Turners—and set it aside. "Welcome home. You just get back?"

"Serena's in the car. She checked her voicemail as soon as we landed and lo and behold, there's a message from Gloria asking why no one had told her you were moving." Micah's scowl etched lines in his forehead. "As you can imagine, we were both wondering the same general thing."

Jonah rubbed the back of his neck. He'd been avoiding calling his friend in D.C. As much as he missed cooking real food, the more he thought about going back to the city, the more his stomach hurt. "It's not a firm decision yet."

"That's sure not what Gloria thinks." Micah crossed his arms. "What's going on?"

"Go home, Micah. You've got to be tired from traveling. Serena's out in the car. Just let it ride, okay? I'll talk to you tomorrow at the bakery." Maybe by then he'd have some idea what to say.

"Seriously? How long have you been a part of this family?"

"Too long." Jonah winced as the words slipped out.

Micah's expression turned to stone. "I see. In that case, I guess I will go."

"Micah, wait." Jonah pushed the footrest down and stood, striding after his brother. "Hold on. You know I didn't mean it like that."

"Oh, really? How did you mean it? I get it. We're always in each other's business. Sometimes it's a royal pain in the rear. But I always remind myself it's because we care—really care—about one another." Micah jerked open his car door. "If you can't see that—don't understand that? Then maybe you should move to D.C. Who knows, maybe Melissa will take you back. I'm sure her latest relationship has ended badly by now."

The knife cut straight through Jonah's heart, just like Micah intended, most likely. His blood began to heat. "You have no right—"

"*I* have no right?" Micah snorted. "That's rich, man. You know what? If you're gonna leave, just do it. If you can't see what you have here, then maybe we're all better off without you."

Micah slammed the car door and tore out of the driveway like a rocket. It was a minor miracle he didn't leave tire marks in his wake. And also a good thing the road leading to Jonah's house was generally empty.

Jonah watched his brother speed off into the evening and sighed. Was it really so wrong to want to get back to the career he trained for? His shoulders sagged. He could try and spin it that way, it wasn't as if there was no truth to it, but if he was honest with himself he'd have to admit it was only the tiniest piece of the puzzle.

Gloria.

Jonah went back inside and picked up his book. She was divorced, sure. But that meant what? In two years they could start dating? Wasn't that what conventional wisdom said? Wait two years after a divorce before dating? How was that any help at all? Two more years loving her and being unable to do anything about it was pretty close to the best definition of misery he could imagine.

No. He couldn't sit around pining for Gloria another two years. And it was clear he wasn't able to stay in Arcadia Valley and move on. Which meant D.C.

Didn't it?

"Mal's out sick today, you're going to have to run deliveries when the baking's done." Micah slid muffin tins into the oven and glanced over his shoulder at Jonah.

"Why can't you do them?"

"Because I'm not the one leaving, which means I'm in charge."

Jonah frowned. "I'm still here. I'm pretty sure you're not in charge yet."

"Just do the deliveries. There aren't many today. A couple of houses in town and L'Aubergine."

"Micah. I—"

"I'm not ready to talk about it yet. Neither is Mal."

"Mal knows?"

"Of course he knows. We stopped by last night after I talked to you. The only person who doesn't know is Ruth, because I'm not going to be the one who ruins her day when she's spending all her time in the NICU with our nephew." Micah took a bowl down from the shelf and set it on the counter.

"Look. My mind isn't as made up as it sounded. I don't know what to do." Jonah ran a hand through his hair. "This thing with Gloria is killing me. I've been trying to get over her, really trying, for three months. If anything, I want her in my life more today than I did in December. So I thought a change of scenery might be just what I needed, you know?"

"Sort of. Serena said she's divorced now, though. Doesn't that change anything?"

"I just found out yesterday. And I don't know if it does or not. Isn't the standard advice that you should wait at least two years before dating and remarrying? So you have time to grieve or whatever? I can't face two more years of her right in front of me but completely out of reach."

Micah blew out a breath. "Maybe. But it's not like Gloria had a normal marriage. She's been estranged from this guy for how long? Like eight years, right? Surely she doesn't need two more."

Jonah shrugged. How was he supposed to know? "I guess someone needs to ask Gloria."

"Someone." Micah laughed. "Not someone. You. You need to talk to her. Until December, the two of you talked about everything. Constantly. Then the whole thing with her marriage happened and it's like the whole communication structure between you disappeared. How many of your problems could've been avoided if you'd just kept talking?"

It wasn't completely his fault. Sure, he'd contributed to the problem, but it wasn't as if Gloria was forthcoming either. "I'll take that into consideration."

"Do that. You can do all your over-thinking while you're out making deliveries."

Jonah sighed. "Fine. But don't think you're in charge for real. Turns out, after having to pull your weight as well as my own, I could do with a little time outside the bakery."

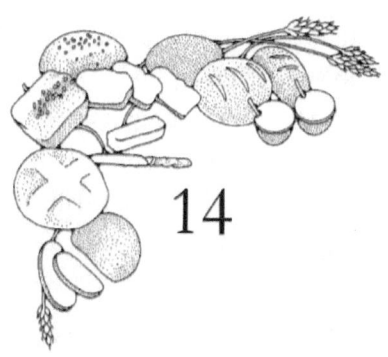

# 14

Gloria carried two large to-go cups of coffee up the stairs of Serena's deck and tapped on the glass door.

"Hey. Oh, you're a life saver. We were planning to stop and get some groceries on our way home from the airport, but your voicemail kind of derailed that."

"Sorry."

Serena waved off Gloria's apology. "That's not what I meant. Come in and tell me everything."

Gloria sipped from her cup and followed Serena inside. She flopped onto the sofa and sighed. When Serena had called, it had seemed like a good idea to come by and unload. Now? She had no idea where to start.

"So?" Serena settled at the other end of the sofa and tucked her legs under her. "What's going on? Any idea why Jonah's suddenly leaving?"

Gloria shook her head. "I kind of think it's because of me. Like I said in the voicemail—I did tell him about the divorce."

"Finally."

She nodded. Serena wasn't wrong. "I'm trying to do better. It hit me yesterday—too late, I realize—that secrets were part of our problem. But maybe it's too little, too late? If Jonah's leaving?"

"You don't know anything more?"

"Micah didn't say anything?"

"He was so mad, I didn't push. He doesn't get angry like that very easily. I don't know if it was the shock or if there was more behind it, but Micah was still stewing when he left for the bakery this morning. Mal didn't take it very well, either."

Gloria winced. "You told Malachi?"

"Micah drove to Mal's after he confronted Jonah. Mal apparently goes the other direction when he's upset, because he got more and more withdrawn as Micah spoke. Or shouted, as the case actually was. It didn't bother Malachi, but Ursula and I were happy to escape to the kitchen." Serena cradled her coffee in her hands. "This is going to kill Ruth."

"Do you think he's committed? Is there a chance he'd stay? I—I could probably transfer to another department. I hate to think he'd leave Arcadia Valley just to get away from me." Her stomach twisted. She didn't want to leave. This was her home now just as much as it was his. But Arcadia Valley was a small town, and the likelihood of avoiding him successfully for any amount of time was slim.

"No. That's not the right solution either." Serena sighed. "I still think the right solution is for the two of you to end up together."

Gloria's cheeks heated. "I'd love that. Now that it's actually possible? I'd give anything to make it happen.

But he has to be on board with it, too. And if he's planning to leave, I'm not sure what I'm supposed to do about it."

"Seriously? Fight for him."

"How? It's not that I'm opposed to fighting, but what am I supposed to do?"

Serena drummed her fingers on her knee. "You told him you were free. Maybe the next step is to make sure he understands that means you're interested—and ready—for a relationship with him. You are, right?"

"Yeah. You don't think I need to wait? All the books—"

"Pfft. Those books are talking about going from arguing to separated to divorced in six months to a year. When was the last time you had any sort of feeling about your marriage beyond resignation?"

Gloria took a long drink of coffee and tried to sort through her thoughts. "A long time. Years. Probably at least five."

"I still don't really understand why you didn't divorce him." Serena held up a hand. "I know, you were going by that whole First Corinthians thing. And I think that's admirable, sort of. But I'm not convinced you didn't take it to an extreme."

Gloria shrugged.

"Anyway, if you feel like you're ready, I don't see the problem. Which means all you need to do is convince Jonah."

"Oh, is that all?" Gloria laughed. "Piece of cake."

Serna grinned. "I believe in you. You've got the whole Baxter clan in your corner, too, which is nothing to sneeze at."

"Thanks. Any suggestions on what step one of this master plan should be?"

"I bet if we put our heads together, we can come up with something."

Gloria smiled. Serena's optimism was contagious. Maybe, just maybe, there was a chance. *Please, God. Let this be Your will. And if it isn't, make that clear. I don't want to go against what You'd have me do.*

Wednesday morning, armed with a list of ideas she and Serena had written out the day before, Gloria stopped by the bakery on her way to the police station to start her shift. They weren't open yet, but Serena had promised to get Micah to unlock the front door so she could sneak in.

Gloria slowly tugged on the door and grinned as it opened. She slipped through, being careful to avoid rattling the bell, though it gave a small ding. Hopefully it was noisy enough in the kitchen at the peak of their morning's baking that no one would notice. Or maybe Micah could keep Jonah from investigating.

She crossed to the cash register and set down a little basket of rosette cookies. They were the only dessert she was particularly adept at, and she'd spent entirely too much time the night before digging through her cupboards for the rosette iron she'd known was lurking in there somewhere. It was the most useful wedding gift her mother had given her, and one of the few things she'd kept. The light, fried dough dusted with powdered sugar was supposed to be a Christmas treat, but Gloria figured there was no law against making them out of season. She should know. She was a cop.

Smiling at herself, she adjusted the note and the bow, said a little prayer, and tiptoed back out of the bakery. She longed to hide somewhere and spy on Jonah's reaction, but aside from needing to get to work, the plate glass windows across the front of the bakery made it nearly impossible. Gloria checked the time and winced. She needed to hurry if she wasn't going to be late to work.

At the station, she changed into her uniform and strode to the desk where a pile of paperwork was waiting for her. Joy. "Hey, Felipe."

Felipe raised a hand in greeting and nodded toward the mass of folders. "Did you lose a bet?"

"I wish. Didn't you get the memo?"

Felipe shook his head.

"Apparently, despite having filled out reports the same way for the last eight years, I've been doing them wrong. Presumably others have as well. But all the forms for the last five weeks have been kicked back to get fixed and re-filed."

"Your tax dollars at work." Felipe cocked his head to the side. "You look happier than you've been in a while. Did you have that conversation we talked about?"

"Oh, yeah. That didn't go quite as well as I'd planned."

"Oh?"

Gloria's licked her lips as she glanced around to make sure the room was still mostly empty. She perched on the edge of Felipe's desk. "He might be moving back to D.C."

"That's not good. So why are you happy?"

"Because I have a plan to convince him to stay. And the support of his family. I'm praying that between the seven of us, we can make him see that leaving would be nothing more than running away. He's supposed to be here, Felipe. Even if he'd not going to end up with me, this is where he belongs."

Felipe nodded. "You know I'm a big believer in being near family. What is your plan?"

"I'm going to court him."

Felipe laughed.

"What?"

"You are serious?"

She nodded.

"Huh."

"Serena thinks—and I kind of agree—that he's probably thinking he can't make a move until some amount of time passes. I mean, everyone knows after a divorce there's supposed to be all this time for healing. And in a normal situation, I'd totally agree. But Frank and I have been over since I moved here. I grieved those first two years—you remember?"

Felipe nodded.

"I don't feel like I need any more time. And I feel like Jonah is someone God wants in my life."

"Ah ha."

"Yeah. So." Gloria shrugged. "I'm going to see if I can help him see that and get him to consider the possibility that staying in Arcadia Valley is about more than hanging out near his siblings. That there might be a life—a full, rich life—for him here, too."

"I'll be praying it works out. Keep me posted?"

"You know I will. Pray for this paperwork, too." Gloria shook her head and settled behind her desk. "'Cause I'd just as soon not get buried alive underneath it before I have a chance to tell Jonah I love him."

Gloria hummed quietly as she turned into the parking lot in front of the bakery. Twice in one day was a new record. Of course, the first time she'd been sneaking. Now she was going to keep it light and breezy. Friendly.

Micah grinned as she entered. "Hey, Gloria."

"Hey. How's it going today?"

"A little quieter than usual, actually. What can I get you?"

Gloria frowned. Was Jonah not going to come out? She stuffed her hands in her pockets and eyed the display cases. "Anything new this week?"

"There's a tomato basil bread that's really tasty, if you want to try it. I can scare up a sample loaf and I'm pretty sure we have butter in the back. Or there's a *dulce de leche* donut."

Gloria pointed a finger at him. "You're trying to hold out on me. Although, the bread sounds good, too. I'll take a loaf of that home. But only if you let me pay for it."

"Just this once." Micah chuckled and rang up her order before scooting down to collect the items and put them in a bag. He leaned closer and whispered, "Those cookies this morning were delicious. He's been trying to figure out how to make them all day. That and wondering who left them. Did you know you didn't sign the note?"

Her stomach sank. She'd packaged up the cookies, written down a rather cheesy poem on the card and her mom had called half-way through. "Oh, no."

Micah nodded. "I think he suspects it's you. I've heard him muttering. But next time, sign the note."

"Yeah. Got it. I can't believe—" Gloria broke off when the door leading to the kitchen swung open. "Hey, Jonah."

"I thought I heard your voice." His gaze lingered on her face longer than usual. Gloria's cheeks heated. "What're you getting?"

"Micah said the *dulce de leche* donuts were good. It's hard to turn down caramel. And the tomato basil bread." Gloria offered Micah her credit card and reached for the bag. "Thanks."

"Got time for some coffee?" Jonah crossed to the mugs and started to fill one.

Gloria checked her watch. "Couple of minutes, sure."

"Micah, why don't you see what Mal's up to?"

Micah's eyes sparkled with mirth as he handed Gloria back her card. "See you later, Gloria."

"Bye, Micah." She headed to the coffee station and reached for a mug.

"I'll get it. Why don't you have a seat?"

He was so close. Gloria resisted the urge to step a little closer. It was already as if electricity sizzled between them. She moved to a table and sat, reaching into her shopping bag for the donut. "What prompted the caramel?"

He smiled slightly as he placed a mug of coffee in front of her. "You've been on my mind. It's your favorite, right?"

"Yeah." Gloria cleared her throat. "I apparently forgot to sign my note this morning."

"Those were from you?"

She nodded and bit into the donut, creamy caramel oozed out of the dough and she caught it with her tongue.

"Those cookies are really good. How do you make them?"

"Maybe I'll show you sometime." She took a big gulp of coffee as the radio on her shoulder squawked. Gloria angled her head to listen before draining the rest of the mug. "I've got to run. These are amazing. You should make them again."

If she wasn't running to a call, she'd probably laugh at the confused expression on Jonah's face. Day one of courting Jonah was definitely a success.

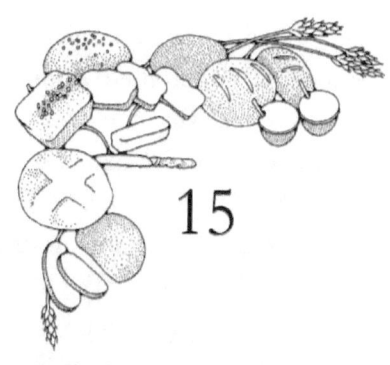

# 15

Jonah set the game console controller aside and sighed. What was Gloria doing? Those cookies had been delightful. But they were fried, and dealing with hot oil wasn't something he was keen to start up. Honestly, he'd be frying donuts instead of baking them if he was willing to bother with that whole process. Frying donuts opened up a lot of options that were close to impossible when baking. He'd been surprised the caramel filling had worked as well as it had today. Filled donuts, in general, were a challenge.

He still hadn't called his friend in D.C.

The couple of times he'd started to call, something had come up and he'd put his phone aside, telling himself he'd get to it later. Maybe it was God trying to tell him something.

Jonah sighed and dug the note that had been attached to Gloria's cookies out of his pocket.

> *Donuts are sweet*
> *Cookies are too.*
> *I never daydreamed*
> *Until I met you.*

He smiled. They'd had so many conversations over the last two years about their hopes and dreams. Gloria had never really had any. She was convinced that dreams were for other people. When had that changed? Certainly not when they met. Recently?

He'd built enough daydreams around a life with Gloria to fill a book. Maybe two. But he was tired of waiting. At some point, wasn't he supposed to move on with things and realize that dreams were just that? Not all dreams came true.

The doorbell rang.

Jonah frowned and set the note aside. Who'd use the doorbell? Not any of his siblings or their spouses. They all just walked in. Gloria, too, for that matter. She was basically already a member of the family.

He'd have to think about that more later. Much later.

He pulled open the front door and blinked. "Morgan?"

"Hi." The gorgeous chef/owner of L'Aubergine crossed her arms as if she was hugging herself. "I hope you don't mind me dropping by?"

"Not at all. Come on in." So many questions raced through his mind. She'd likely answer them once they were inside. "Can I get you something to drink?"

"No. I'm fine, thanks." Morgan looked around. "I haven't ever been inside here before. Been driving by for forever, but Corban and I never ran in the same circles."

Jonah gestured to the couch and resumed his seat in the recliner, shifting Gloria's note to the side table.

"You're welcome any time. I'll make sure you get invited to the next party we have. I'm sure once Ruth's back home and settled with the baby she'll be itching to have another to-do."

"I hear good things about those. Mostly about the food, which, I understand, is primarily your doing?"

He nodded. "Everyone pitches in, but yeah, I guess."

"When you first moved here, you asked if we were hiring and, at the time, we weren't."

At the time? Jonah nodded. "I'd say that worked out for the best, given how well A Slice of Heaven is going."

Morgan gave a weak smile. "Yeah. And I hate to even suggest what I'm about to, but I really don't know what else to do, short of closing down L'Aubergine."

"Close down? Is business really that bad?" Last he'd heard, it was still sometimes a challenge to get a reservation at the popular local restaurant. On any day of the week.

"Not business." Morgan pressed her lips together and stared at the ceiling for a moment. "It's me. I have breast cancer. They're saying I need radiation and chemo and that it's going to be at least a year of treatment. Everything I've read says that I'm going to be too exhausted to run a kitchen while I'm being treated. If I had an office job, or something more flexible, then maybe...but you know what a chef's life is like. Throw in all the business management on top of it? I just don't think it's reasonable to expect to be able to continue. So,

I thought it was better to be proactive and figure something out before it was an emergency. I've been praying about it for two weeks and the only name that comes to mind is yours."

"Mine." Jonah struggled to absorb everything she'd said. "Cancer. That stinks. I—you're asking me to take over L'Aubergine for a year?"

"Maybe a little longer. Call it eighteen months to be safe." She held up a hand when he opened his mouth to speak. "I don't think it'd actually interfere with the bakery. You do most of the baking in the morning, right?"

He nodded.

"We can close for lunch. I'd been toying with that—or at least cutting back to one, maybe two days a week—anyway. No one wants fancy candlelit lunches, and I don't see the point in trying to compete with all the places that do casual lunch around here. Our niche is fancy dinners out."

"Hmm." That changed the situation considerably. Just doing dinner made it tiptoe into the realm of plausible. "Prep for dinner starts at what, one?"

"About, yeah. We can adjust dinner hours, if you needed a little extra time. Right now, we're taking reservations that start at five. We could bump that to five thirty, maybe six if we had to."

"I don't think you need to do that. By one, I'm generally done with all the baking and clean up. Even with special orders. I spend the afternoon either helping out up front, making flour, or prepping a little for the next day. Most of that Micah can easily handle, even with manning the cash register. Mal can pitch in with some of it too, if push comes to shove." Jonah drummed his fingers on his knee. "Let me pray about it and talk to my brothers. When do you start treatment?"

"I have to have surgery first. They want to schedule it as soon as they can. I know I'm not going to be able to cook while I'm recovering, but the guys can probably hold things down a few days if they have to."

"I'll let you know by Friday."

"You sure two days is enough time? I don't want to rush you."

Jonah chuckled. "I'm pretty sure my siblings are going to think this is an answer to their prayers."

Morgan shot him a confused glance.

"Not your cancer, obviously. I've been talking with a friend in D.C. about moving back to help run his kitchen. They don't want me to go."

"And this would keep you here. For a while, at least." Morgan's smile was a little wider this time. "There really is silver lining in every rain cloud, isn't there?"

"I'm sorry you're sick."

"Me, too. But as cancer goes, I'm glad it's this and not something that doesn't get so much research and attention. The survival rates for breast cancer are so much higher today. I'm not making light of it, but, all things considered, my only big worry has been the restaurant." Morgan stood and held out a business card. "I put my cell on the back. Call me when you have a decision?"

Jonah took the paper and rose as well. "You bet. I'll be praying for you."

This time, Morgan grinned. "Thanks."

After walking her to the door and watching her back out of the driveway, Jonah returned to the living room and his recliner. He set Morgan's cell number next to Gloria's note. *Okay, God. I think maybe I get the hint.*

Jonah poked his head out into the front of the bakery. "Hey. Got a minute?"

"Sure." Micah stood and stretched his back. "Need me to come back there?"

"No, I'll grab Mal. Maybe fix us all some coffee?"

Micah's eyebrows rose, but he said nothing.

Jonah strode through the kitchen and peered into Malachi's tiny office. He waved to get his brother's attention before signing his request for Mal to join them out front.

Malachi frowned, clicked a few times on the computer, and stood.

"It's a little early for Gloria, isn't it?" Micah smirked up at Jonah from one of their small round tables. He'd pulled a third chair over and put steaming mugs of coffee at each seat. "Though I do appreciate you leaving the flowers she gave you out front. Several of our customers have commented on how lovely they are."

Flowers. She'd sent him flowers from Blossoms by the Akers. Yesterday it had been a tiny box of chocolate hearts. "This isn't about Gloria."

"It should be. You're being an idiot. The woman's smitten and if you can't tell that, you need your head examined." Even Malachi's sign language oozed grumpiness.

Jonah sighed. Mal hadn't vocalized anything to him since he'd mentioned maybe leaving. He still signed—there were things that had to be communicated and Mal was too much of an adult to give him the full silent treatment—but Jonah was so used to listening to his brother, he hadn't realized how often he looked away during a conversation. And right now Mal wasn't repeating anything he signed when Jonah wasn't looking, no matter how nicely he asked. "I think, maybe, what I have to say is going to make you happy."

"Yeah? How's that?" Micah sipped his coffee, hesitated, stood and walked behind the display cases. He dropped three sugar cookies onto a plate and returned to the table.

"On Wednesday, Morgan Taylor stopped by the farmhouse."

"Do you even hear yourself? 'The farmhouse,' like it's some kind of local site instead of your home. Why not just call it your house?" Micah broke a piece of cookie off and dunked it in his coffee.

"Because it's not my house. It's Corban's house. He just lets me live there." Jonah shook his head. "Could you stop being mad at me for one minute so I can explain?"

"Fine." Micah pushed the plate of cookies toward Malachi.

"She asked me to take over as chef at L'Aubergine for the next year, year and a half while she has chemo."

"Is she okay? Obviously she isn't. Will she be?" Micah dropped the rest of his cookie on the table. "Can we help her somehow?"

"I don't know. She seems to think she'll be fine after treatment, just not up to running a restaurant during. Which makes sense. So she asked me and I told her—"

"No." Malachi signed and rolled his eyes. "Why are we having this conversation?"

"I told her I'd pray about it and talk to the two of you. It'd mean I'd have to leave here around this time every day to start dinner prep. There are some kinks that we'd need to work out, but I think it's doable. My heart says it's the right move, but I wanted to talk to you guys before deciding for sure."

"That's a nice change." Micah picked up his cookie. "Your job in D.C. still gonna be there in eighteen months?"

Wow. He hadn't realized just how badly he'd hurt his brothers until now. Jonah wrapped his hands around the mug of coffee in front of him. "No. If I do this, I stay here. Permanently. No more running away."

"And Gloria?" Mal asked, his hands folded in his lap, silent.

Jonah fought a smile. At least one of the twins had forgiven him. Or was willing to. "Seems like by the time I'm finishing up at L'Aubergine, enough time should've passed that Gloria and I can see where things take us."

"Pfft. What are you waiting for? The woman is practically courting you." Micah pointed at the cheery mixed bouquet on the counter. "Or did you not notice?"

"That doesn't mean she's ready for a relationship. She's only been divorced what, two months?" Jonah reached for the remaining cookie. He didn't really want it, but he needed to do something with his hands so he didn't reach across the table and throttle Micah. Why did he not see how hard this was?

"That's just the legality. You talk to her? Seems to me she's been divorced a lot longer than that in all the ways that matter." Malachi reached for his coffee. "I think staying is good. Helping out at L'Aubergine is doable. And you need to get your act together and tell Gloria you love her and quit messing around."

"I'm working up to that, okay?" Jonah's face heated. He was. Sort of. "One thing at a time. Are the two of you okay with me telling Morgan I'll help out?"

"Of course." Micah glanced at Malachi. "We can handle the afternoon, right? Especially if we keep the two high schoolers. When Serena starts filming it may get a little trickier, but I don't have to go visit as often as I was hoping. We'll figure it out."

"You sure?" Jonah glanced at his brothers.

Malachi nodded.

"Thanks, guys. For what it's worth, I'm sorry I didn't talk to you more about leaving. I wasn't as serious about it as it seemed. I was just—"

"Running away?" Micah sipped his coffee.

That wasn't how Jonah would've phrased it, but maybe the shoe fit better than he was willing to admit. "Yeah, okay."

"I'm glad you figured it out before you did something stupid." Micah grinned.

Malachi laughed. "Can we get back to work now?"

"Yeah. Go. I need to call Morgan and tell her we're set. I may start trying to hop over there as soon as next week. It'd be good to have some transition while she's still around."

"Keep us posted, we'll figure it out. Right now, Serena doesn't have any idea when filming is going to start. There was some kind of hiccup that had her on the phone with her agent for hours yesterday. At this point, I'm beginning to wonder if she wouldn't be better walking."

"She turning down other offers?" Jonah stuffed the last bit of his cookie into his mouth. They were a little dry. He'd work on that.

"Not yet. But since she's been clear that she's only doing one a year, I suspect her agent is nixing stuff before even showing it to her. I don't want her to miss out on something she'd really enjoy because of hassles with this project."

Jonah laughed. "Listen to you, all Mr. Hollywood."

Micah rolled his eyes. "I just want her to be happy."

"I suspect she's good there. She has you." Jonah's gaze flitted over to the vase of flowers by the cash register. Could he really have that with Gloria?

"Call Morgan. Then call Gloria. Maybe the two of you should sample the cuisine at L'Aubergine before you take over."

Jonah nodded slowly. "I like the way you think."

Jonah smoothed a hand down his tie and tried not to frown. How had he not known these apartment buildings were here? And that they were so...ramshackle. That was the only word that came to mind. Why did Gloria still live here? Surely she made enough to get one of the little houses in town, like the one Ursula and Mal lived in. Ursula had bought it on her own long before she and Malachi met. Maybe Gloria just liked the convenience?

The butterflies in his stomach were practicing for some sort of dance competition. As many times as he'd asked Gloria out over the last two years, he hadn't expected nerves when she finally said yes.

He grabbed the half-dozen roses from Blossoms by the Akers off his passenger seat and crossed the parking lot, making his way to Gloria's apartment. He knocked on the door and held his breath.

Gloria opened the door. "Hi."

She was wearing a dress. It was a simple, short-sleeved black dress, but it hugged her curves in all the right places and stopped just north of her knees. Jonah snapped his mouth shut and swallowed. "You look...wow. Um. These are for you."

Gloria took the roses, her cheeks pinking as she buried her nose in them. "Thanks. Want to come in for a minute while I put them in water?"

He followed her through the door and stopped. The living room and kitchen were fully visible from the entry. A little hall poked off to the right leading, no doubt, to her bedroom and the bath. It was a straightforward apartment, not unlike the one he'd had in D.C. Although his apartment there had been in better shape. Housing prices there were such that run down generally wasn't allowed to happen.

"There." Gloria set the roses, now in a tall vase, in the center of her kitchen table. "Ready?"

Jonah nodded and held out his hand.

She studied it a moment before slipping her hand into his with a smile and grabbing a little clutch purse and teal wrap from a tiny table by the door.

He tried to ignore the electricity fizzling up his arm and his scrambling heartbeat. "Have you eaten at L'Aubergine before?"

"Sure. Sometimes the higher ups will have a gift card that they give out for good work. I've won a few times. And Felipe and Constance have taken me and a small group out on their anniversary. They always say it's more fun to celebrate with friends than alone."

Jonah chuckled. "I'm not sure I'd agree with that."

"Right? Maybe when you've been married as long as they have it's different. I'd think any night you can get a sitter and get out of the house is a good one though." She shrugged.

Jonah held the car door for her before zipping around to his side. There was a vague element of disbelief that hovered on the fringes of his mind. He glanced over. No, it wasn't a dream. Gloria was really sitting there, waiting for him to start the car. "I'm glad you were free tonight."

Her eyes sparkled with laughter. "I'm glad you called. I have to admit, I thought it might take longer."

"What would take longer?"

"Getting you to realize it'd be okay to ask me out again. I have another two weeks' worth of plans. And even then, I thought I might have to ask you."

He put the car in reverse and backed out of the parking spot. What was he supposed to say to that? "I didn't want to rush you. After a break up..."

"And I appreciate that. I do. But Jonah? Frank and I were over so long ago. If you'd showed up the first two or three years I was here, then, sure, I wouldn't have been ready. But I made peace with the end of my marriage a long time ago."

"Not enough to actually do the ending though."

Gloria winced. "Ouch. Though I suppose that's a fair point. I never had peace about being the one to initiate it. I prayed about it so many times and felt like the answer was always to just wait. I don't know why. Especially when there was no miraculous restoration. When you did show up and I realized I was falling for you, it gave me some hard moments. What kind of person falls in love with another man when she's still married? Even if the marriage is just a technicality?"

In love? He risked a glance at her before pinning his eyes back on the road. Did she realize what she'd said? "It's tricky, to be sure. I had similar questions in December."

"I imagine you did. I'm sorry to have put you in that position."

"You didn't. You never did anything untoward or out of line for someone who was married. I read a lot of things as more than friendship when you clearly hadn't meant them that way. I'm glad, at the end of the day, that we ended up with a solid friendship anyway."

It was a good foundation to build more on. His parents had always stressed the importance of friendship with your spouse. That was one of the things he and Gloria had that Jonah had never really had with someone he dated. Now they had time. Even if Gloria was hinting that she didn't need it—he wanted to give her time to heal. To be sure she was over everything. He could take it slow.

"Maybe." She sighed and looked out the window. "I just pray that somehow God will use this whole situation to bring Frank to faith in Jesus."

Jonah nodded and pulled into the parking lot at L'Aubergine. "I'll pray for that, too. As long as it doesn't mean you'd want him back?"

She shook her head. "I'm not in love with him anymore. I'm not sure what we had was ever more than hormones and proximity."

"Okay." He glanced at the restaurant, admiring the quiet, cozy feel that even the parking area exuded. "Ready to go in?"

"Absolutely. I'm surprised you got a reservation so easily at short notice."

He smiled, taking her hand in his again. Nothing had ever felt so right before. He sent up a quick prayer of thanks. "That's an interesting story. Why don't I tell you over dinner?"

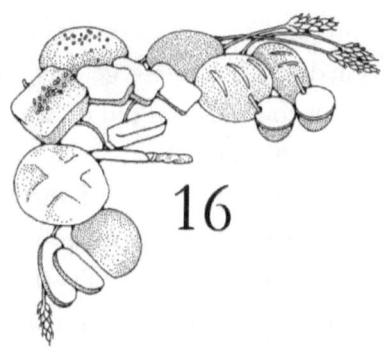

# 16

"Tell me all about it, don't skimp on the details." Serena grabbed Gloria's arm and pulled her out of the line at The Beanery.

"Am I booking you for assaulting an officer now?" Gloria glanced longingly at the line which would, eventually, get her coffee. Coffee that she needed desperately if she was going to make it through the Saturday shift that got sprung on her at 6 a.m. when Miller called in sick. Coffee she needed *now*, which was why she'd stopped at The Beanery rather than crossing town to visit the bakery.

"Cranky. Hmm. That's not a good sign. The date wasn't good?"

Gloria groaned. "The date was fine. I need coffee. And I'm on duty. How'd you find me, anyway?"

"Seriously? It's not hard. I called your cell, it went to voicemail so I knew you were on duty. Then I just had to look for a cruiser. Cause you're the only one who routinely visits the shops while serving and protecting."

"No, I'm not. Everyone stops in when they're on patrol." She sighed. "Can I please get my coffee? Then I promise you I'll tell you all about dinner with Jonah."

"Fine. I'll grab a table."

Gloria walked to the back of the line. She'd be three people closer to glorious caffeine if Serena hadn't grabbed her. Throw in that she wasn't sure she *wanted* to spill all the details of her date with Jonah. It was still a warm memory that she could pull out and replay just for herself. Would sharing it with Serena make it lose that shivery edge? She inched forward. It was too late to weasel out of it, most likely, and that was adding to the general grumpiness of her sleep-deprived morning.

When she finally had her coffee in hand, she found Serena and sat. "Why didn't you get something?"

"I had some at home. Come on. Details. Was it everything you hoped it would be?"

Gloria hadn't had any particularly huge expectations. "I don't even know what that means. It was nice."

"Nice? That's all I'm getting?"

She shrugged. "I don't know how to do this girl gushing thing, okay? He picked me up, looking even more amazing than usual in a tie and sport coat. We ate at L'Aubergine which, as you know, is always an incredible experience. And for the first time since probably August, nothing was stilted or weird between us."

"Did he kiss you good night?"

Gloria shook her head, frowning. "It was our first date."

"After three years! You two are going to be sixty by the time you get around to getting married."

"He held my hand."

Serena angled her head to the side, her eyes lighting up. "Ah ha. So there were sparks."

"You knew there would be. I'm not sure he's convinced he's ready for sparks. Or he's not convinced I'm ready for them. Something was holding him back." It had been the only tiny damper on the evening. As much as she'd like to say she wouldn't have kissed him on the first date, the reality is she probably would've. Happily. "So I'll keep on with the plan. Clearly it's working."

"That's it?"

Gloria sipped her coffee. "What do you want me to say? Am I glad he asked me out? Absolutely. Did it go well? Yep. Do I think we'll go out again? I hope so, but I'm not sure."

"Okay, sorry. I had this vague idea that he'd sweep you off your feet. I forgot for a moment that you're not someone who's willing to be swept."

Gloria frowned. That wasn't true. Just because she wasn't the girliest woman on the planet didn't mean she didn't want to have romance. "I should get going."

"Tell me one more thing?"

She sighed and scooted out her chair. "What?"

"What'd you wear?"

"It was L'Aubergine. I wore a dress."

Serena's eyebrows lifted. "You?"

"It's been known to happen. I'm sorry my date was a disappointment to you. I'll see you later. I need to roll."

"Gloria."

Gloria shook her head and strode from the shop. Serena meant well. She probably didn't even realize how insulting the whole conversation was. Well, maybe she'd gotten the picture when Gloria walked out. It would be nice to be able to share stuff like that with friends. Maybe something in her was missing? Did it all tie back to not being as girly as it seemed like other females were? At least it hadn't ruined her memory of the date. She could still savor the evening and call up the sensation of Jonah's hand in hers.

That brought a smile to her lips. Hopefully that was an experience she'd get to repeat sometime very soon.

Gloria hovered in the doorway of the sanctuary. She didn't normally sit with the Baxters. Was it presumptuous to think Jonah would want her to today? It wasn't like they hadn't offered before, but making it to church on time was an iffy proposition for her. It was better to plan on slipping in the back when she could make it. She should just grab her usual spot and—

"Hey, you made it." Jonah's hand glided down her arm from elbow to wrist leaving shivers in its wake. "I wasn't sure if you'd have to work today or what. I planned to call you after and see if you could at least swing by the house for lunch with everyone."

Everyone. For a moment there, Gloria had glimpsed a quiet lunch at his house, just the two of them. Of course, the Baxters always ate lunch as a family. It was one of the things she loved about them as a clan. "I traded shifts. I've got a double later this week, but I wanted to see you."

The smile bloomed slowly on Jonah's face and he slipped his hand in hers. "I know how that feels. Come on, we should get a seat."

Gloria followed as he tugged gently on her hand. Malachi and Ursula grinned and scooted down a little to make room. It was still weird not to see Corban and Ruth sitting with the family. She leaned closer and whispered in Jonah's ear, "Any word on when Ruth and Corban will be home?"

He nodded. "Maybe two weeks. At this point, they're just waiting on weight gain. Once he's closer to what his birth weight would likely have been, he should be able to regulate his temperature outside the incubator. That's the last major milestone they're waiting on."

That was good news. Gloria opened her mouth to speak, but the band got into place up front and invited everyone to stand for worship.

Her gaze kept drifting to Jonah next to her as they sang. It was always an experience to watch him at church. Not that she'd made a study of it. At all. He had a way of losing himself in his singing, and even though his hands stayed at his sides, he looked as though he should have them raised in the air with abandon. Had she ever worshipped like that? Maybe. There was a little part of her that wondered how much she held back from God the way she tried to hold pieces of her heart back from the people she loved. But if she didn't give them her whole heart, they couldn't destroy her completely. Wasn't self-preservation allowed?

As the singing continued, Gloria's eyes filled. She blinked back the tears as God broke through the last walls around her heart. Self-preservation might work well in the short term, but long term? Long term required surrender. If she was going to have the relationship she craved with Jonah—or with God—she needed to choose to trust. Trusting Jonah was easy. Trusting God was harder. She'd paid lip service to that trust for a number of years. Now it was time to fully surrender.

The rest of the service passed in a blur. Gloria's thoughts were scattered. Somewhere during the sermon, Jonah had inched his hand over and closed his fingers around hers. The contact was a quiet, solid anchor to the present.

When the benediction was finished and quiet piano music started up, Jonah turned, curiosity written in his features. "You all right?"

She nodded. "Yeah."

"You'll come for lunch?"

Something in Gloria's chest loosened. "I'd like that."

He grinned. "Great. See you soon?"

"Absolutely."

It took several minutes to work her way out of the sanctuary. It seemed like everyone wanted to stop and chat today. Glancing over her shoulder, she saw the Baxters had managed a cleaner escape. Ah well, that just meant lunch was more likely to be ready when she arrived. Finally, she extricated herself from the friendly overtures that, today, seemed overbearing and unwarranted, and made her way to Jonah's.

At the front door, she paused. Should she knock or had she moved past that somehow? Spock smiled at her from the foyer, his tongue lolling out one side of his mouth. That was enough invitation. Gloria slipped through the screen door and paused to scrub the faithful dog's head before making her way into the living room.

Malachi and Ursula stood facing one another in front of the fireplace, their hands moving at lightning speed. From Ursula's stony expression, their conversation wasn't a pleasant one. Should she...uh oh. Malachi glanced in her direction and froze, his glare slowly morphing into a strained smile.

"Everyone's in the kitchen. You can go on back."

Ursula crossed her arms. "Or you can tell Mal he's being an idiot."

Whoa. Definitely not getting involved in a fight between married people. Gloria held up her hands and backed up. "I'll just be going."

"Coward." Ursula hurled the word at her.

"You know it, sister," Gloria muttered under her breath as she backtracked into the kitchen.

Micah and Serena were moving dishes to the table after Jonah filled them.

"Hey. How can I help?" Gloria fought the urge to reach out and brush Jonah's arm—anything that would return that pleasant sense of belonging she'd had in church that Malachi and Ursula had shattered.

"They still fighting?" Jonah jerked his head toward the living room.

"Yeah."

Micah shook his head. "Maybe we should—"

"Oh, no, we shouldn't." Serena reached for Micah's hand. "They're adults. Married adults. They'll figure it out."

"I take it nobody knows what the problem is?" Gloria reached for the bowl of salad Jonah grabbed out of the refrigerator.

"Nope." Jonah shrugged. "After you get that on the table, would you prop the tablet up against the chair at the end of the table?"

Gloria's eyebrows lifted. "Sure."

Serena took the bowl and pointed to the tablet.

It took a couple of tries to get the thing balanced against the back of the chair so it wouldn't slip back down onto the table. "What's this for?"

"Ruth and Corban." Jonah smiled and carefully tapped on the screen, bringing up a video conferencing app. He raised his voice and hollered, "Hey you two, lunch is served."

After a minute, Ursula and Malachi joined them at the kitchen table. They took their seats, not looking at one another.

Gloria's heart clenched. Married people fought. She got that. It was hard work to be in a relationship, but those two were still basically newlyweds. What could be causing that much discord? Her gaze flicked to Jonah who watched his brother and sister-in-law carefully.

"You two okay?"

Ursula sighed.

Mal gave a hesitant nod.

Jonah waited a moment before poking a photo of Ruth on the app. Ringing was the only sound for several seconds before Ruth and Corban filled the screen.

"Oh, yay! It worked." Ruth grinned and waved. "Gloria! You're there, too?"

"Yeah. Hi. It's neat that you can sort of join us for lunch." Gloria smiled.

Ruth's eyes narrowed. "Are you and Jonah finally together?"

Gloria's face heated.

Jonah cleared his throat. "She agreed to go on a date with me. Beyond that, we haven't really—"

"Yes." Gloria swallowed, her gaze flicking to Jonah's and holding it. "If he still wants that, we are."

One corner of his mouth curved up. "Really?"

She gave a single nod.

Everyone around the table broke into applause and cheers.

"It's about time." Ruth beamed at them through the screen of the tablet. "We have some good news of our own."

"Yeah?" Serena leaned in until her picture appeared in the small window that showed what the tablet camera was picking up. "Do you get to come home soon?"

"Next week." Corban slipped his arm around Ruth and kissed the top of her head. "They said he's doing great and barring any setbacks, we'll be released on Saturday."

Gloria's eyes filled. What amazing news. "God is so good."

"He really is." Ursula turned to Malachi, her eyebrows lifted.

He closed his eyes and gave a small nod.

"We have some news of our own." Ursula cleared her throat. "I wanted to wait a little longer—but I'm pregnant."

"What?" Jonah jumped to his feet. "Congratulations! Why would you wait with news like that?"

Malachi gestured for Ursula to speak. Her cheeks turned pink. "I miscarried once already. Two months after we were married. It was super early, I'd barely found out I was pregnant. But it still...it hurt."

"Of course it did." Serena crossed her arms around her middle and leaned into Micah. "Why would you go through that alone?"

"We didn't want to...it just seemed like..." Ursula faltered and glanced at Mal.

He scooted closer to Ursula and wrapped an arm around her shoulders. "Sorry."

"You know better. Both of you." Jonah frowned.

Ruth nodded. "What he said. But there'll be time to berate you later. Today is for celebrating."

Gloria's eyes found Serena and she hurt for her friend who had been in an accident that took the life of her husband and their unborn child, leaving her infertile, before she came to Arcadia Valley. Serena wore a smile, but the signs of strain were there for those who could see them. Pregnancy announcements were hard enough for her, but talk of losing a baby, too? What must she be feeling?

Serena met Gloria's look and her smile grew slightly. She mouthed, "I'm okay."

Micah rubbed Serena's shoulders, the two of them just slightly apart from the excited conversation that washed over the table.

Gloria glanced over at Jonah. His eyes locked with hers and he reached over and took her hand. He leaned closer, his breath tickling her ear as he spoke. "As exciting as their news is, I'm happiest about what you said."

Her mouth went dry as her heart picked up speed. She turned slightly, a smile on her lips. "Me, too."

It was Wednesday before Gloria had time to track down Serena. Now that Jonah had taken over the kitchen at L'Aubergine, it wasn't as if she was going to go to the bakery for her usual afternoon break anyway. Not that Micah and Malachi weren't always happy to see her, but it wasn't the same. Why was it that now she and Jonah were together they never seemed to have time to see each other?

She knocked on the door to Serena's pottery studio before entering.

"Hey."

Serena looked up and offered a tired smile before taking her hands off the clay spinning on her wheel and letting it come to a stop. "Hey yourself. What brings you out this way? Shouldn't you be serving and protecting?"

"I am. I'm on a break." Gloria searched her friend's face, noting the signs of sleeplessness. "You're not okay."

Serena sighed. "Let's go in and grab a drink. Maybe a break's not a bad thing."

Gloria waited while Serena washed her hands, then followed her friend back to the house.

"Soda? Or water? I haven't had time to make tea or anything lately."

"Water's fine. I'm over caffeinated today as it is." Gloria perched on a stool at the kitchen island. "Want to talk about it?"

"No." Serena filled a glass at the tap and handed it to Gloria before snagging a soda from the fridge and popping the top. "I'd much rather talk about you and Jonah. Has he kissed you yet? How was it?"

Gloria pressed her lips together. "Not yet. Do you really want me not to push?"

"I don't know." Serena rubbed her hands over her face and lowered herself onto one of the other stools. "Micah keeps trying to get me to talk about it, too. I don't know what to say? I'm happy for her—them. I really am. But it also feels like a little part of my soul has been ripped out and shredded. I know what she's going through, those first weeks of pregnancy, but because of the accident I'll never get to say those words to Micah. And it breaks my heart."

Gloria swallowed, her own heart breaking as tears slipped down Serena's cheeks.

Serena swiped at them with the back of her hand. "He says it doesn't matter. And maybe it doesn't matter to him. But it matters to me. And then I feel small and ridiculous, because really, I'm making this all about me when it's not about me at all. She miscarried. I know what that loss is like. But I can't see past my own heartache to go to her and tell her that the pain will fade eventually. It doesn't go completely away. At least, it hasn't for me. I'll always wonder about that baby. But it's not so raw after some time has passed."

"I'm sorry." Gloria gripped her water glass with both hands. Maybe coming here was a bad idea after all. It wasn't like she had experience to share. All she could do was try to understand and empathize. And neither of those things were her strong suits.

"Yeah, me too. He really hasn't kissed you yet?"

Gloria shook her head. Maybe it was time to let the subject change.

"What's wrong with him?"

She laughed. "Not all of us kiss on our first date, you know?"

"Please. The two of you have been out so many times already, you're on like the nine thousandth date. Have you done the lean in and let your eyes drift half-closed thing?"

Gloria snorted, trying to picture just how ridiculous she'd look trying that. "Do you know me at all?"

"Sorry. Forgot who I was talking to for a minute." Serena drummed her fingers on the counter. "Okay, so Gloria fashion. Hmm. That's more along the lines of 'Hey. Are you gonna kiss me or not?'"

"I'm not that bad."

Serena's eyebrows lifted. "On a scale of one to ten, how often does he see you in something other than your police uniform?"

Ugh. She hunched her shoulders. "That's not fair."

"Right. So when you're in cop mode? What I described is exactly how you are." Serena lifted a shoulder. "But apparently he goes for that, so you might as well use it to your advantage."

"Thanks. Thanks a lot." Gloria drained her water and stood. How had a visit to her friend to try and be supportive turned into a critique of all the places she failed as a girly girl? "I should get back to all that serve and protect stuff and leave you to your pottery."

"Gloria?"

"Yeah?"

"Thanks. I really do appreciate it. I'm going to be okay. But you might need to remind me of that every now and then." Serena stood and slung her arm over Gloria's shoulders. "I know you're not a hugger, so humor me, okay?"

Gloria laughed and gave Serena a fast hug. "I'll make an exception just this once. When you need that reminder? You have my number. Any time of day. Got it?"

Serena nodded.

Gloria gave her a quick salute before clomping down the deck stairs to her waiting cruiser. She'd made a lot of the first moves in her relationship with Jonah—at least once she was free to pursue it. Did she need to nudge him along a little faster in the kissing department?

She caught her lower lip between her teeth. Her imagination could do a lot with the idea of kissing Jonah. It was something she definitely wanted to experience— sooner than later—but maybe she could find a way to send him a hint rather than walking up to him and laying it on the line. She could be softer, more feminine, when she needed to.

A line from a poem flirted just outside of her mental reach. She'd do a little poking when she got off shift and see what she could come up with.

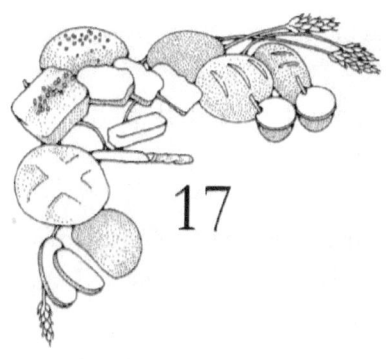

17

Jonah cracked open the seal on an ice-cold water bottle and drained half of it in three long swallows. Prep for the dinner service was finished, finally, and they had about fifteen minutes before the first reservations were due to arrive. Morgan had a solid team in her kitchen. Why did she think she needed him? Maybe none of them were particularly creative, but surely they could execute the menu as written? They'd done a good job the past three nights.

Morgan's surgery was scheduled for today. Hopefully it had gone well. Would she let him know? They were casual acquaintances at best, even if she had asked him to take over the kitchen in her absence. He shrugged it off and finished the water.

"All right, gang. You ready?"

The two line cooks nodded and made a few last-minute adjustments to their stations.

Jonah left the kitchen and walked briskly through the three dining rooms, double-checking that everything was ready. The front-of-house team was just as solid as the back. Maybe Morgan was too much of a control freak.

He stopped by the desk at the front door where the manager waited with the hostess. "I think we're set. Any issues?"

The manager winced. "We're down a server. Juliet called in at the last minute. Again. I think we're going to need to let her go."

Juliet. Jonah sorted through the blur of faces that made up the wait staff. "High school senior?"

"Yeah. With a new boyfriend. I'm guessing her illness is more love sickness than anything else."

"That's hard. See if you can get a replacement before you let her go. I'll double-check with Morgan, but I'm pretty sure she'd agree."

The manager nodded. "That's my feeling. Just know the servers are going to be scrambling to cover the tables and get food out."

Jonah blew out a breath. "Get me a copy of the table layout. I can run food if it starts to pile up."

She blinked. "You'd do that?"

He shrugged. "Why not? Food's better when it's hot. I'd rather run some food than have to redo it when it's sent back for being cold."

"All right. Thanks. I'll try to keep it from becoming a habit."

Jonah chuckled. "Do that. We stay busy back there, but we're all on the same team, right?"

"Right." The manager glanced at the hostess. "Let's open up."

Jonah turned and headed back to the kitchen. It was good to be surrounded by something other than the smell of bread all the time. Knowing the kitchen awaited him in the afternoons made his mornings of kneading and baking fly by. The only potential problem was, of course, that he was burning the candle at both ends. He was up and baking by five each morning and didn't fall into bed until after midnight. It left him no time for anything remotely resembling a personal life.

Just when he finally had one.

He sighed and pictured Gloria on Sunday at the kitchen table. He could almost feel her hand in his, her eyes locked with his, electricity zinging between them as she corrected him in front of everyone. Together. A couple.

At last.

A server bustled in with a ticket. Jonah took it, cleared his throat, and called out, "Here we go."

The night was zipping by. So far the wait staff had done an admirable job keeping up with their extra tables, but now he had five dishes waiting for pickup. "Guys, I'm going to run this food before it dies. How are we doing?"

"Four minutes out on the four-top, six for the next two-top."

That was enough time. Jonah grabbed the plates, balancing them precariously since he didn't see a tray handy, and pushed through the kitchen door into the main dining area. The four-top was table sixteen. He closed his eyes and pictured the chart before heading across the room into one of the smaller areas.

"Good evening. Who had the filet?"

An older woman Jonah vaguely recognized from church raised her hand. Was her name Nancy? Pon...something. Someday he would get better with names. He set the plate down and went through the rest of the table, pleased that he hadn't gotten the location wrong. The single plate was in the back room, overlooking the garden. He wished the diners a good evening and passed through the doorframe, stopping as his gaze landed on Gloria.

"Hi."

She grinned up at him. "This is a nice surprise."

"I think that's my line. What are you doing here?"

"Eating dinner. Is that my stuffed eggplant?"

"It is." He set the plate down and reached for her hand. "It's really good to see you."

"I was going to ask to speak to the chef. I didn't realize they'd downgraded you to food delivery."

Jonah laughed. "One of the servers called out, it was all starting to pile up, we had a minute so...in the end, I think it worked out pretty well. For me, at least."

"I won't keep you. I just wanted to see you, even if it was only for a minute. I'm sure you're slammed back there. Thursdays look almost as busy as Fridays, though I did manage a same-day reservation, so that's something." Gloria squeezed his fingers before pulling her hand from his. "Get back to work."

He'd never wanted to get back to the kitchen less in his life. "I wish I could sit with you."

"I promise to order dessert. Go on, I don't want to be responsible for other people not enjoying their night out simply because I needed to see the man I love."

Jonah's mouth opened but no words formed. That was twice now. Did she mean it?

Gloria sent him a soft smile. "Go. Text me later. I might be up."

He nodded and went back to the kitchen, his brain still turning circles. She hadn't told him she loved him, so it wasn't as if he could've said, "I love you, too." But at the same time, shouldn't he have had some kind of response? Something beyond a slack-jawed stare?

He was losing it. Badly.

"Hey, boss, you have trouble out there? Got orders piling up." The line chef nodded toward the little stack of written orders left by servers.

Jonah pulled himself back into the present and forced down the desire to run back to Gloria's table and declare his love. This wasn't the time or the place. "Where are we with the four and the two?"

"Ready for the final check."

"Okay, here we go." Jonah rattled off the new orders, slid the tickets in line, and finished the plates for the completed dishes.

The man she loved.

The man who loved her.

*Thank you, Jesus.*

Jonah glanced at the clock as he kicked his shoes into the corner. Nearly one in the morning. There was no way Gloria was still up. Was there? They'd had two tables that kept ordering long past the time when the kitchen was supposed to close. He'd finally gone out to give them a little hint that it was time to move along since the manager didn't seem to be making much headway. They were up from Twin Falls where they were vacationing. As much as Jonah loved that they'd heard about Arcadia Valley and all its charms, he'd wanted nothing more than to get home and text Gloria.

He grabbed a glass of water and tapped on the phone as he climbed the stairs toward his bedroom.

"Hey. Imagine you're asleep. Was good to see you though."

Jonah hit send and tossed the phone on the bed while he stripped off his clothes and dropped them into his overflowing hamper. He was going to have to make time to do laundry before long. In fact...he eyed the clothes and shrugged. There was no point in pretending he was going to sleep in the next hour. Might as well get a load started.

Jonah pulled on pajama pants, not bothering with a shirt, and hefted the hamper. After a moment of deliberation, he grabbed the phone and dropped it in a pocket. There was no way Gloria was still up. But if she was, he didn't want to miss her reply.

He'd just closed the lid on the machine when the chime sounded. Probably a spam email. Those always seemed to come in the middle of the night. He spun the dial and got the cycle going before reaching into his pocket.

His heart fluttered in his chest. A text.

"Late night. Everything okay?"

He grinned and hit call.

"Hey."

"Is it okay to call? I guess I should've asked first."

She chuckled. "No, it's good. I'm gonna be beat tomorrow, but I'll survive. That's what God made coffee for."

"Tell me about it. I'd forgotten how wired a dinner shift leaves you. I've been running on about four hours of sleep a night. It's not a sustainable model."

"Ouch. No, it isn't. What are you going to do?"

Jonah passed through the kitchen and stretched out on the sofa in the living room. "I don't know yet. When Micah's in town, he can get started with the baking on his own, but the bread is really more my specialty. And it needs time to rise. I could maybe get it mixed and started rising after I leave the restaurant, but that might be too long, and it still puts more bread work on Micah's shoulders than he wants. We'll figure something out."

"I don't suppose you can make it the day before?"

"Nope. Fresh bread is our thing. I don't mind so much the muffins and cookies if we're in a pinch—and we've had to do that a couple of times when Micah disappeared to visit Serena—but not the bread. Day old bread simply isn't the same. We'll figure it out." Jonah tugged the throw off the back of the couch and pulled it over him. Should he mention the love thing? How was he supposed to work that into a conversation? Even if he could, wasn't it better done in person? "Thanks for coming by tonight."

"I'm glad I got to see you. It's not the same with you away from the bakery. I miss you."

Warmth that had nothing to do with the blanket washed over him. "I miss you, too. I'm off Sunday. And Monday. Any chance I could see you? Like a date?"

"I'd like that. A lot. I think I'm working Sunday. I traded shifts a few weeks ago and I think it's catching up with me this weekend. Monday for sure I'm off. What do you want to do?"

He hadn't gotten much past asking her out before his thoughts leapt down paths that were probably better left unexplored. "Um. I haven't looked to see what the weather's like. We could go for a hike down by the Snake River? Take a picnic maybe?"

"That sounds perfect."

Jonah yawned, his jaw cracking as it stretched wide. "Sorry. Maybe I should try to sleep after all. If you can swing by in the morning, I should still be at the bakery. I know it's a shift in your routine, but—"

"Worth it. I'll see what I can do. Not sure why that didn't occur to me." Gloria chuckled. "Maybe I'm more tired than I thought."

"Go to sleep. I'll see you tomorrow, hopefully." He shifted, getting more comfortable on the couch. He'd just doze here until the washer was finished. "'Night."

"Good night." She drew in a breath and hesitated, as if she had more she wanted to say. Jonah waited, chastising himself for not having brought up their conversation at the restaurant. Maybe she would?

The phone went dead.

Jonah sighed and ended the call. Coulda, shoulda, woulda. He'd see her tomorrow. Maybe that was soon enough.

"Why don't you go home and take a nap?" Micah slid the stack of sheet trays onto the shelf where they were stored and looked around the kitchen. "The baking is done and it's only nine thirty. You could get two, maybe three hours of sleep before you have to be at L'Aubergine. You look like you're dead on your feet."

That was an accurate description. Jonah leaned against the counter and rubbed his gritty eyes. He'd fallen asleep on the couch after talking with Gloria and hadn't awoken when the washing machine buzzed. The alarm on his phone had barely caused him to stir. "Yeah. Maybe. It's just—"

"Hold that thought." Micah grinned and darted out into the public area of the bakery.

Had the door chimed? Jonah hadn't heard it if it did. He should take his brother up on the nap. Exhaustion, sharp knives, and hot stoves were a bad combination. He crossed to the little office and waved at Mal, signing, "I'm heading out. You okay?"

Malachi nodded. "All good. Get some sleep. You look like death."

Great. Jonah made a face and waved. He'd go out through the front and maybe he'd bump into Gloria, or at least see her. She hadn't said it was for sure that she'd be by, just that she'd try. And as much as he wanted to see her again, spend even five minutes with her holding her hand, he could use the sleep more.

He pushed the door open and strode into the bakery proper. He clapped Micah on the shoulder. "I'm gonna take your advice and head home. If—if Gloria comes by, would you explain?"

"Sure. But she hasn't been by all week. She knows you're at the restaurant."

Jonah nodded. "I talked to her last night. She was going to see if she could make it in the morning."

"Ah. Sorry, man. You have to be at the restaurant at what, one?"

"About that, yeah. Why?"

"Need me to call around twelve thirty and make sure you're up?"

Jonah blew out a breath. He'd set an alarm but... "That's not a bad idea. Thanks."

"You got it." Micah made a shooing motion. "Go. Get that nap."

"I might make a stop along the way. Could you box up a half-dozen cookies?"

Micah raised his eyebrows but dug out a small box and started filling it. "What kind of stop?"

"At some point over the past two weeks, once I started to see that things with Gloria actually had a chance of working out, I realized I probably owed Kenia an apology."

"Um. You sure? It's not like you purposefully led her on."

"No. I know that. I think she probably knows that. But the fact remains that it wasn't fair to her to try and start something when my heart belonged to someone else. I'm grateful she recognized it before we wasted too much time." Jonah shrugged. "It's a small town. I can't avoid her forever—don't even want to, if I'm honest. She's a great girl. And Page Turners is a great shop."

Micah laughed and handed Jonah the cookies. "Tired of shopping online?"

"That's not the only reason."

"Relax. I'm teasing you. I'm not sure there's anyone who'd say you *had* to apologize to her, but I think it says a lot about you that you want to. Mom'd be proud."

Jonah smiled. Mom absolutely would be proud. Of course, she'd have kicked his butt for dating Kenia in the first place when he'd known his heart was still tied up with Gloria. But he'd been trying to move on.

"Go. Make your amends and then get some sleep before you fall over in the middle of walking somewhere."

Jonah laughed, offered his brother a sketchy salute with the box of cookies, and headed toward his car. He wanted to wait for Gloria. On the other hand, when was he going to find time to apologize to Kenia if he didn't take it now? This was the smarter choice. He needed sleep more than he needed to see Gloria.

Monday.

If he could make it through the weekend, they had a date on Monday. That would have to be enough.

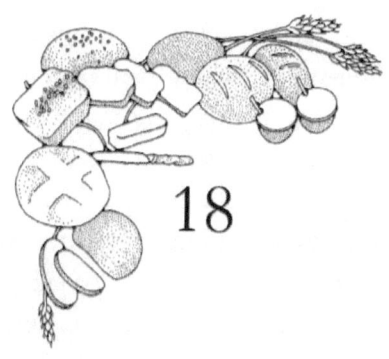

18

Gloria pulled the cruiser into Jonah's driveway and cut the engine before reaching for the brown paper sack she'd carefully belted into the passenger seat. She strode quickly up the front steps, pausing to rub Spock's ears, and pushed the doorbell. She counted to ten and pushed it again, then knocked on the door. That last was Micah's suggestion. Jonah, apparently, slept like the dead. She could hear a phone ringing inside and grinned. That was Micah's contribution to the plan. She pushed the doorbell a third time.

"Hang on."

Gloria held back a laugh. He sounded like a petulant toddler.

The door swung open. "Wha—oh. Hi."

"Grumpy when you wake up. That's an interesting little fact to have possession of." Gloria held up the bag. "I brought lunch."

"Yeah?" He scrubbed a hand over his face and stepped back. "Come on in. Maybe head to the kitchen, I should go change."

Gloria nodded, filing away the image of Jonah in a snug black T-shirt and pajama pants covered with space ships for later. In the kitchen, she rummaged through the cabinets until she had bowls and plates, then poured soup from its insulated container and arranged sandwich halves. It wasn't a presentation worth of L'Aubergine, but it was better than letting him eat out of takeout boxes.

He was back before too much time had passed, dressed for the restaurant, his hair wet where he'd slicked down the cowlick that his bed-head had revealed. "This is nice. Thanks."

"I stopped by the bakery—but it was nearly noon. Micah explained that you'd gone home to sleep, so I figured lunch might not go amiss. Gotta eat, right?"

He nodded and reached for her hand. "Right. But this is above and beyond. Thanks. You have time to eat with me?"

Gloria pulled out a chair but kept a hold of his hand, enjoying the shivers it sent up her arm. "Unless my radio goes off, yeah. It's slow today. It's slow most days, that's why I love it here."

"This smells amazing. Where's it from?"

"I didn't want to take a lot of time, so I buzzed into Benita's. They have a little deli area at the back of the store. I've always liked their soup."

"Huh. Who knew?" Jonah squeezed her fingers. "Can I pray?"

"Of course."

"Father, thank You for this meal. But mostly, I just want to say thank You for Gloria and for letting us spend some time together today. You know how much I wanted this—thanks for the blessing. Amen."

Her cheeks heated. Had anyone ever thanked God for her while she was sitting there? Certainly not that she could remember. She cleared her throat. "How are you feeling? Did the nap help?"

"You know what? It did." Jonah dipped his spoon into the soup. "Mm, this is pretty good. It needs cheese though. You want some?"

"Cheese?" Gloria tasted the soup. What would cheese do to it? On the other hand, she wasn't a chef. And cheese...was it ever a bad idea? She shrugged. "Sure. Why not?"

He stood and dug through a drawer before opening the fridge and emerging with a small container. He sat down and pried up the lid to remove a white chunk. "Parmesan."

Who kept real Parmesan in their fridge? She had a bottle of powdery stuff that claimed it was Parm. It tasted fine on spaghetti, and really that was all that mattered. She smiled as he ran the block over the microplane, shaving flecks of cheese into both bowls of soup. "You really are a foodie, aren't you?"

He laughed. "Guilty. But I don't consider it a bad thing. Give that a stir and see if you don't think it's better."

Gloria did as instructed, blinking when she took another taste. "Wow. All that from a little cheese."

"To be fair, this is amazing cheese. And it's salty, so it's doing double duty." Jonah took another bite and nodded. "Much better. From Benita's, you said? Maybe I'll pop in if I get a chance and suggest it. Benita and I are friendly enough I think she'd take it okay."

"The sandwiches probably aren't up to your exacting requirements. I usually dunk them in the soup." Gloria hunched her shoulders. Maybe bringing lunch was a bad idea. She was no cook. Sure, she could throw together a meal, but she'd always considered Benita's a step up from anything she managed.

"I'm sure they're fine. And I appreciate not having to make my own lunch. If you hadn't come by, it would've been PB&J in the car on the way to the restaurant, if anything." He reached for her hand again.

"Are you sure?" Serena was likely to have something pointed to say about the flop of her first attempt to do something like this. Just another check mark in the "unfeminine" column. "I'm not what anyone would call skilled in the kitchen. This is at least as good—probably better—than anything I'd be able to make on my own."

"That's okay. I like to cook. Even when I'm not working. And not every meal has to be fancy. Soup and a sandwich is great." He cocked his head to the side. "I'm sorry if you felt I was criticizing you. That's not how I meant it."

"Okay. I'm not girly. It's always been a bit of a problem for people."

Jonah shrugged. "Not for me. I love you the way God made you."

She smiled, her pulse racing. Maybe he had been listening. Not that she'd been quite that straightforward. "Yeah?"

He nodded.

Gloria cleared her throat and dragged her thoughts away from the little flashes of future possibilities that zinged through her mind. "We should probably eat before the soup's cold."

Jonah chuckled and reached for his sandwich. "What's the rest of your day hold?"

"I'm heading back to the high school again. They're really trying to crack down on the speeding problems there. I hate it, but I drew the short straw."

"Sorry. On the positive side, school will be out in what, two months?"

"About that, yeah. Think it'll ease up then?" Gloria grinned and scraped up the last bite of her soup. "What's the special tonight?"

"I don't even know. I've been finding out when I get there each day. Morgan probably has a list somewhere—some kind of plan. I was thinking I'd try and stop by tomorrow morning and see how's she's doing. Drop off some casseroles I threw together."

When did he have time? "You're amazing."

Red crept up his neck. "It's what friends and neighbors do, isn't it? One of the best parts of being in a small town. Plus, the guys at the restaurant all helped, so it didn't take any time. We just figured it was better to have one person go rather than a whole delegation."

"When does she start chemo? Any idea?"

Jonah shook his head. "All I know is she's expecting treatment to take a year."

"Cancer stinks."

"It really does." He reached for her bowl and stacked it inside his. "Thanks again for lunch. It's really good to see you. Would you be weirded out if I said I missed you?"

Gloria chuckled. "No. 'Cause I missed you, too. We're still on for Monday, right?"

"Barring catastrophe, absolutely. Can you swing lunch on Sunday? Ruth and Corban and the baby should get home tomorrow, and they're planning to have everyone over at the B&B. I'll cook, obviously, but they've missed the big family dinner."

"I should at least be able to stop by, yeah. I'm glad they're finally getting home. Right about his due date?"

"Yeah." Jonah stood and carried the dishes to the sink, Gloria followed. He turned and nearly bumped into her. After a moment's hesitation, he slid his arms around her waist and pulled her close, lowering his forehead to hers. "Have a good rest of the day. Be safe."

Gloria's heart hammered against her ribs. Would he finally kiss her? For a moment, she considered Serena's advice, and then discarded it. That wasn't her style. At all. With her luck, he'd think she was about to sneeze, or something equally ridiculous. She wrapped her arms around him and snuggled closer, basking in the warmth and electricity of the contact. "I love you, Jonah."

"I love you, too." He pressed his lips to her forehead before he stepped back "I should run."

Gloria fought a stab of disappointment. "Text me when you get home tonight? I can't promise I'll still be up, but if I am, I'd love to hear from you."

"You sure? It's Friday so it'll probably be a little later than—well, it'll be more like last night when we ended up open later than usual."

"I'm sure. I don't keep my phone in the bedroom, so if I'm asleep, I won't hear you. If I'm not, well, then I'll get to chat."

He chuckled. "Deal. Thanks again for the food."

"Anytime." Gloria squeezed his hand, reluctant to let go. She stepped backward, still holding his hand, until she had to let go or drag him with her. Her hand fell to her side and she lifted it in a wave before turning and forcing her feet to take her back out to the cruiser. Duty called. Love would have to wait.

Apparently their frequent speed traps by the high school were working.

Gloria checked the clock in the dash and sighed. Two hours of sitting here, watching kids drive safely and slowly past her. Some of the braver had offered a jaunty wave as they went by. Maybe they were getting started on their Friday afternoon plans with less speed than they wanted, but at least they, and the pedestrians that flooded this area, were all safe. Which was exactly the point.

She shifted in her seat and listened to dispatch sending a unit out to Retro Village. Someone was visiting the retirement home at least once a day. Usually a wrong number, but the police still had to respond. Last week, Felipe had been called out to investigate some stolen dentures. They'd been found in the old man's glasses case. No one had found the missing glasses yet to her knowledge.

She smiled. Small town cop wasn't dramatic or fast-paced, but it was a solid living. She liked the people and the town. It was good to feel like she was doing her part to keep her home safe.

A car zoomed past, rocking the cruiser. She checked the readout from the radar gun mounted on the back of the cruiser and flipped on the lights and sirens, as she called it in. Someone, it seemed, hadn't gotten the memo.

She chased the low-slung red sports car for three blocks until it finally pulled to the shoulder.

Gloria shook her head as she pushed open her door and headed toward the car. Why hadn't they stopped sooner? It wasn't as if Arcadia Valley was somewhere high-speed chases took place. She tapped on the window and waited while it lowered. "Afternoon. Can I see your license and registration, please?"

The young man inside swallowed, his Adam's apple bobbing. Nerves pumped off him, his hands shaking as he offered the requested items. "Sure. Of course."

"You know how fast you were going?" Gloria glanced from the nervous driver to the two teenage girls in the back seat, both of whom were studiously avoiding eye contact. Something was off here. Cops made people nervous. She got that. But generally the folks in Arcadia Valley were ready with a smile. Even when she was pulling them over.

"No, ma'am. I wasn't paying attention. We're late for an orthodontist appointment. I didn't want to end up getting bumped and having to pay the seventy-five dollar fee."

Gloria gave a slight nod and looked down at the documentation he'd provided. His face matched the photo and the names were the same. That was positive. Still. She angled her head to glance at the girls again. "Well, I'll try to make this as quick as possible. You might want to give them a call though. You seeing Dr. Hart or Dr. Obrinsky?"

"Uh. Hart." The driver's eyes searched the area just over her shoulder.

Uh huh. There was no orthodontist appointment. Dr. Hart was great, but she was a local veterinarian. She offered another smile and took a step back toward the cruiser. "I'll just be a minute."

As she walked, she gave dispatch the name, demographic information, and license number for them to begin their searching. Gloria sat and keyed the information into the laptop mounted in her car. The photo in the database matched that on the driver's license as well. Nothing on the car popped. Those girls though. Her gut twisted. Something was sketchy.

The dispatcher called her number.

"Go ahead."

"We got a hit on a warrant in connection with trafficking of minor females. Should we confirm?"

Those two girls. Her heart kicked into overdrive. "Affirmative. There are two minor females in the back seat of the vehicle. Requesting backup."

"Backup's on the way, ETA three minutes. Warrant confirmed."

"Copy that. I'm going to reapproach and attempt to keep him from becoming suspicious." Gloria stared at the computer screen for another moment, working on keeping her features neutral. She didn't want to tip him off. She grabbed her ticket book.

"Everything okay?" The driver made brief eye contact before looking away.

"Yes, sir. I am going to issue a citation for excessive speed. We're in a posted school zone, you were doing nearly eighty." Gloria flipped open her ticket book and lined up the license so she could begin to write.

"I really wish you wouldn't do that."

She flicked her gaze up and froze. The barrel of a Beretta extended through the car window. She dropped the ticket book and reached for her own weapon as everything started moving in slow motion. "Sir—"

Pain ripped through her shoulder, knocking her backward as she screamed. The tires on the car spun, leaving dark stripes of rubber on the pavement as it rocketed away.

Gloria touched her left shoulder and pulled away her hand. Bright red blood dripped from her fingers. Too much. Her vision went gray around the edges as she tried to stumble toward the cruiser, reaching for her radio with her good hand. *Officer down. Suspect fleeing. Officer...*

Gloria dragged her eyes open. Where was she? A face materialized in front of her, lips moving without sound.

Her arm was on fire.

A siren pierced through the bubble of silence that surrounded her, and her eyes drifted shut.

Pressure and pain, like something hard and heavy rammed into her chest jolted her eyes open, and Gloria fought for breath.

"Sinus rhythm. And we're here. Let's go."

Bright light made her squeeze her eyes shut. She tried to focus on the words being flung around and over her, but the screaming pain in her shoulder was louder than even her own thoughts.

"...stopped the bleeding..."

"...two jolts..."

"Get her to surgery..."

The jostling motion of whatever she was on combined with all the noise made her head swim. She closed her eyes and let the blackness take her.

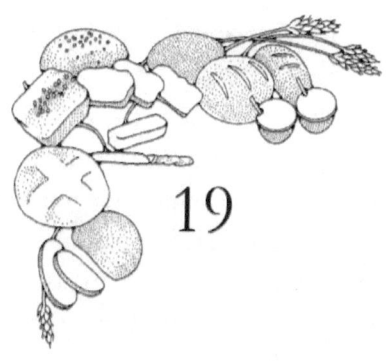

19

"Jonah. You're here."

He looked up from the onion he was dicing as he and the two sous chefs prepped for dinner at L'Aubergine. "Morgan? Of course I'm here. Why are you?"

She clasped her hands in front her, her knuckles white. "I was on my way out to the car when an ambulance came tearing in."

"Let me get you a chair. You don't look good. I'm not sure you should be here. Did you drive yourself?"

"No, my dad brought me. He's out front. Look, you don't understand."

Jonah scooped the onion into a container and dropped it in the prep area. He wiped his hands on a towel. "I'm going to get you a chair, and then you can explain."

He went out into the restaurant proper and snagged the first chair he saw, lifting a hand in greeting to Morgan's dad who chatted at the hostess stand with the manager.

"Here. Sit. You need a drink? Some water or something?"

Morgan lowered herself to the chair and swallowed. "No. Jonah, the ambulance."

"Right. At the hospital." He managed to avoid rolling his eyes. Where else would an ambulance be? That's what they did, they took people to the hospital. And okay, sure, emergencies were never fun. But if one of his brothers or their wives were injured, they would've called him.

"It was a cop. I think it was Gloria, I'm fairly certain I heard them saying the name Sinclar—I might've made Dad roll us closer to see what the fuss was."

His stomach dropped into his shoes and he shook his head. "Can't be. We just had lunch. It could've been anyone."

"How many women are on the force?"

Two? Three? He swallowed against the bile that crawled up his throat. "No. Look, I'll call her and you'll see."

Jonah fumbled for his phone and hit dial. It rang. And rang. And rang. Her voicemail picked up. That didn't mean anything. She could be busy writing a ticket or in the restroom somewhere. Something. Anything. His breathing was shallow. He couldn't get the air he needed. He hit end and punched call again. "It's not her."

"Jonah..."

He held up a hand as the phone went to voicemail again. He cleared his throat. "Hey, Gloria. Gimme a call, would you? Just real fast? Please?"

"You need to go."

He stared at his phone, willing it to ring. "I can't. Dinner—"

"The guys can handle it. I can stay and—"

"No. You're white as a sheet. You just had major surgery. You need to be at home, in bed. It's not her, anyway. Can't be." His phone still wasn't ringing. Why wasn't it ringing? He swallowed again. "I know. I'll call the hospital."

Morgan shook her head.

Jonah tapped out a search in his phone's browser and hit call for the displayed number.

"Arcadia Valley Community Hospital."

"Hi. Um. I wanted to check on the status of a patient? Gloria Sinclair?"

"Sir, we can't give out patient information on the phone."

"But she's a patient?" His pulse drummed in his ears.

"I can't give out that information over the phone, I'm sorry. Can I help you with anything else?"

His heart sank. "No. No thank you."

"Well?"

"They won't say. Felipe. He'd know." Jonah drummed his fingers on his thigh. How was he supposed to get a hold of Felipe? Serena? Would she know? He scrolled to her contact and hit send. She picked up after five rings. "Serena?"

"Hey. Sorry, I was in the middle of a tricky part with a commissioned vase. What's up? Shouldn't you be prepping at the restaurant?"

"Yeah, long story. Do you happen to have a way to get in touch with Gloria's friend Felipe?"

"Felipe? I might. She gave me a list of emergency contacts at one point when she was feeling morbid."

Some of the tension in his muscles flowed away. "Think you could find it and get me his phone number?"

"Sure. Can it wait 'til later?"

"I'd rather not. Do you mind?"

Serena gave an exasperated grunt. "The two of you tiptoe around each other for nearly three years, now you're finally together and suddenly everything's an emergency? Give me ten minutes. I'll text it to you."

"Thanks."

"Yeah, yeah."

His phone went dead and he winced. One ticked off sister-in-law? Check. And since Gloria wasn't in the hospital, it was going to be for nothing. Unless...his gaze flicked over to Morgan who watched him, concern evident on her face.

"Well?"

"Serena's getting me the number. Then we'll see." Jonah's hands trembled slightly as he set the phone aside and reached for a bulb of garlic that needed to be peeled and minced.

"Don't."

He stopped, his hand on the hilt of his knife, and stared at Morgan.

She gave a mirthless chuckle. "You'll cut a finger off. Or worse. And while that's one way to find out if she's at the hospital, I'd just as soon you weren't injured because of me."

Jonah rubbed his face, his eyes stinging as the onion juice on his fingers found its way into them. "Yeah, all right."

"Why don't you just go? The guys—"

"I'm not going down to the hospital to make a fool of myself unless you're positive it was her." Jonah grabbed his phone as it buzzed. Serena was fast, he'd give her that. And he'd owe her for taking time out of her work to look it up. "Here we go. Now we'll see."

Felipe's phone rang and went to voice mail. Jonah hung up and dialed again. This time, Felipe picked up on the second ring. "Hello?"

"Hi. This is Jonah Baxter. I'm not sure how to explain this without it being weird, but—"

"Jonah. Thank God. How did you hear?" Felipe's voice was strained and Jonah clearly heard the hospital PA system in the background.

This couldn't be real. Everything around him seemed to echo. "My friend, Morgan, was leaving the hospital when the ambulance arrived. I don't understand. What happened?"

"Gloria was shot."

Jonah stumbled back a step, bumping against the counter. That didn't happen in Arcadia Valley. It just didn't. He gripped it until the edge bit into his palm. "Is she? What—How?"

"We do not have many answers. She's in surgery right now. They said it could be a couple of hours."

"Can I come?" Jonah looked around the kitchen without seeing. He needed to be here. He'd promised Morgan. But Gloria...what was he supposed to do? He couldn't lose her just when he'd finally found her, could he? *Please God, no.*

"Yeah. There are four of us in the waiting room on the surgical floor. Could you bring food? It will be dinner soon and no one wants to leave, not even to head down to the cafeteria."

He managed a slight smile. He'd raid the bakery. He wanted to stop and tell Micah and Mal anyway. They could tell their wives. Ruth. Then they'd all be praying. "Of course. I'll be there in maybe thirty minutes. Thanks."

"I'm sorry." Morgan started to stand, but Jonah waved her back into her seat.

"I have to go. I don't know what to do about dinner service."

"Like I said before, the guys can manage it. We'll tell people when they arrive, and if they want to cancel and reschedule, we'll give them a discount for later. Go."

"You should be at home, resting." Dueling obligations tore at his heart.

"I'll leave soon. Promise. You go to Gloria. Call me when you know something though, okay? I'll be praying."

"You're sure?"

Morgan growled. "Go. Before I fire you to solve the problem."

"Okay. Thanks." Jonah grabbed his phone and jogged out the back door, his mind racing. If she was in surgery, he should really stay, at least help with the prep. It wasn't like he'd be able to do anything productive at the hospital. And yet, everything in him was screaming to get there. It was almost physically painful to consider any other action.

The short trip to the bakery was a blur. He parked in front and dashed in. "Can you pack up like four loaves of bread and whatever we're nearly out of? I'll be right back."

Jonah caught a glimpse of Micah's confused expression as he dashed back out and down two doors to Benita's market. He zipped through, grabbing some of the cured meats she stocked, as well as some cheese, condiments, and a sharp knife. They'd make sandwiches. It'd give everyone something to do while they waited.

"What's going on?" Micah was loading cookies into a box when Jonah darted through the door a second time.

"Gloria's been shot." His voice broke as a sob caught in his chest. He took a deep breath and pushed it back down. "That's all I know."

Micah froze. "What? She's what?"

"Shot. I know. Can you tell Mal and everyone? Just pray. When I know more I'll text you." He reached for the bag.

Micah shook his head and went back to filling the box. "Let me get you some donuts, too. Who's at the hospital? How'd you find out?"

"Cop friends? I don't know. Morgan was on her way out when she saw the ambulance. She overheard and saw enough she thought it was Gloria and came to tell me. I called Serena to get Felipe's number. She's a little annoyed with me. Can you let her know I wasn't just wasting her time?"

"Of course." Micah handed him a second box. "Don't worry about it. I suspect she'll want to come by as soon as she can. Gloria is her best friend here."

Jonah swallowed. "Yeah. Um. Surgical waiting room. If that changes, I'll let you know. You know what? Let me fill up some to-go cups with coffee, too. Hospital coffee is gross."

Micah snickered. "As we discovered when Ruth was there. Tell you what, you go. I'll make sure Serena brings coffee when she comes."

"Okay. Thanks."

"Keep me posted."

Jonah nodded and hurried his bags out to the car. The hospital was close. His drive there was filled with the only prayer he could muster. *Please, God. Please.*

The food was mostly gone. A few lonely slices of bread were strewn haphazardly on the torn paper bag he'd carried everything in. By and large, only crumbs were left. How they'd managed to eat escaped Jonah. He'd tried to choke down a bite or two, but his throat was tight and his stomach was roiling. It was probably for the best that he hadn't succeeded.

The crowd of cops had thinned as well. Felipe sat next to Jonah, head in his hands, but everyone else had left, some with promises to return, others with demands to be kept informed.

Gloria had a lot of people who loved her.

Jonah checked the time on his phone. "It's been close to three hours."

Felipe nodded.

"Didn't they say two?"

He nodded again, adding a shrug. "They know what they are doing. She lost a lot of blood."

Jonah glanced over, his stomach knotting. "You've been skimpy with the details. Can you tell me anything more?"

Felipe sighed and looked around. "Routine traffic stop gone bad. Guy had a warrant out, she was trying to stall to give backup time to get there. He shot her and took off."

"I thought she wore a vest." Wasn't it standard at this point for cops to have body armor? Why would she be so careless?

"She does. We all do. He missed it—deliberately is my guess. Got her in the shoulder, hit the brachial artery."

"Artery?" Jonah pressed his lips together and fought the nausea that washed over him.

Felipe nodded. "It was a near thing. They said her heart stopped on the ride here from blood loss."

Jonah blinked as his eyes filled. He opened his mouth to ask another question when a tired, rumpled looking man came through the doors that led to the patient area.

"Which of you is Gloria Sinclair's next of kin?" The man's gaze flickered between Jonah and Felipe.

"I am on her emergency contact list." Felipe stood and gestured to Jonah. "This is her boyfriend."

The surgeon nodded. "She made it through surgery. The bullet shattered her shoulder. I think we've got it put back together well enough that she won't need a replacement, but it was intricate work. Barring complications, she should be fine. Lot of recovery yet to go, though."

"Can we see her?" Jonah clasped his hands together in his lap.

"Once she's out of recovery and in a room. I'll send someone out to let you know. Might be another hour before that happens."

"Thank you." Jonah buried his face in his hands and took several deep breaths. She was going to be okay.

"I am going to go call Constance and some of the others, let them know. Are you okay?" Felipe rested his hand on Jonah's shoulder.

"Yeah. I am now."

Felipe smiled. "Make sure you tell your sister-in-law. I'm surprised she left."

Jonah laughed. Serena had stayed for ninety minutes before leaving to help Ursula with an emergency at the B&B. He'd promised to keep everyone posted. So he would. "Will do. Thanks, Felipe."

"We love her too."

Jonah watched Felipe leave then let his head fall back to the wall. He closed his eyes and breathed a prayer of thanks. Life was uncertain. Maybe it was time to grab on to the woman he loved with both hands and never let go.

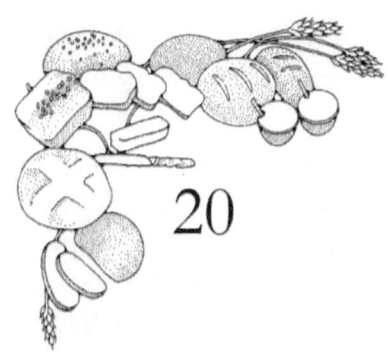

## 20

Gloria pried her eyes open and turned her head. She furrowed her brow. "Jonah?"

"Hey." Jonah leaned forward and gently took her hand. "How are you feeling?"

"Everything hurts." She grimaced. "Why are you here?"

"Where else would I be? Let me call the nurse." He reached for the button and pressed it. "They weren't going to let me stay last night, but I called Emerson and he asked Pam to pull some strings. I figured your reputation was safe enough, seeing as there's no privacy in a hospital room. Please don't be mad...I couldn't leave you."

She smiled at him, her heart warming.

A nurse bustled into the room, a harried smile on her face. "You're awake. How do you feel?"

"Like I was shot?" Why did people keep asking her that? "I'm not sure how I'm supposed to feel."

The nurse grinned. "Scale of one to ten, how's the pain?"

Ten. That's the word that floated through her mind. Then she remembered the pain of the bullet tearing into her shoulder. "Eight?"

"That bad still?" The nurse frowned and checked the IVs hooked to Gloria's bed, fiddling with a few of the tubes. "Here, this button will dispense more pain medication when you push it. It's on a timer, so you can't get too much, but try not to use it unless you need it."

Gloria took the button and pressed it. "How long does it take?"

"Shouldn't be long. Can I get you some breakfast?"

Gloria nodded. She wasn't sure she could eat, but having the option seemed like a good idea. "Thanks."

"No problem. Call or get your young man to come to the desk if you need something." The nurse bustled back out the door.

The edge of the pain receded. Gloria let out a breath and turned back to Jonah. "I'm glad you're here. But what about the bakery?"

"It's Saturday. Lighter day, Micah's got it. I can't get away from L'Aubergine tonight though. So I can only stay until lunch. Serena's going to come by then to spend the afternoon. Felipe called your mom. She's flying in, Ruth and Corban will pick her up in Twin Falls on their way home from Boise." He squeezed her good hand. "You had a lot of people worried about you."

"Sorry." She turned her hand over and laced her fingers through his. "Did they get the guy?"

Jonah nodded. "Felipe said the State Police got him a couple of hours north, looked like they were heading to Canada. The two girls in the backseat are safe. They'd been reported missing in Nevada four days ago."

Her stomach twisted. Those poor girls. What must they have been through? She shuddered.

"Cold? I can get you another blanket."

"No. Just thinking about the girls. You read the reports, but it's not something you expect to touch here. We're a friendly small town, not the city."

"Yeah." He brought her hand to his lips and kissed her knuckles. "You scared me."

"I bet. I understand."

He frowned. "You understand what?"

"That it's too much. Loving a cop isn't for everyone. I don't expect—"

"Stop. I'm so proud of you. So amazed by you. Even if we are a small town with very few problems, you care about people enough to go out every day and face danger. It's incredible. *You're* incredible. Scary? Sure. But it's who you are. I love you. That means I love who you are."

Warmth spread through her. She searched his face, struck by the earnestness in his gaze and the love shining from his eyes. She blinked as her eyes filled with tears.

"What's wrong? Does it still hurt?"

She shook her head, a laugh bubbling out of her throat. "No. It's just you. I love you, too. Thank you for really seeing me. Who I am."

His lips curved. "That's my pleasure. The doctor said you'd have full range of motion after a lot of physical therapy and healing. Felipe's guessing you'll be off work for at least three weeks, then stuck at a desk—his words—for at least three more."

"Sounds about right." Gloria sighed. "Did you say my mom's on her way?"

"Yeah. She should be here around two. Ruth's going to put them up at the B&B. Ursula said she could still pitch in while everyone adjusts to being home. They can stay with you once you get sprung from here, or keep on with Ruth. We can play it by ear."

"The B&B. I don't—there just isn't room in my apartment. Is Harry coming, too?"

"I think so. Serena should have more details when she gets here." Jonah stopped talking as the door opened and someone came in with a breakfast tray.

Gloria reached for the lid covering her food and gasped as it jostled her injured arm. Her eyes watered.

"Let me help you." Jonah stood and scooted the rolling tray closer before removing the dome and unwrapping the utensils. "Do you want to sit up a little more?"

"I guess. Thanks." She swallowed the lump in her throat. This sucked. She didn't want to be in the hospital, injured. She was supposed to be at work, helping keep the streets safe. Providing help, not getting it. Gloria glanced at Jonah who watched her, concerned. "I'm all right."

"Do you want me to leave?"

How awful was it that she wished he'd never come? Never had to see her like this in the first place? Too late now. "No. It's okay."

Jonah glanced at the door then back at Gloria. "If you're good for a minute, I'm going to run down to the lobby where I can get a few bars on my cell and make a couple of calls. Back in ten?"

"Sure." Taking care not to move or jar her injured arm, Gloria reached for her fork. She poked the yellow glob that was, ostensibly, eggs and sighed. At least her pain was receding as the medicine kicked in. Her mother was going to be the first to tell her that this pity party was unattractive and selfish. But still. Wasn't she allowed to wallow for a few minutes? Especially when she threw in the fact that even getting shot hadn't managed to motivate Jonah to kiss her?

At this rate, she'd be on her death bed before he worked up the courage to do more than hold her hand.

"Oh, sweetheart." Gloria's mom dropped a shopping bag at the side of the hospital bed and placed her hands on her hips. "You look dreadful. Didn't you ask someone to bring a little blush? Or lipstick?"

Gloria laughed. "Mom. You know I don't bother with that stuff when I'm healthy. Why would I ask for it in the hospital?"

"I don't know where I went wrong with you."

"Billie May." Harry came to Gloria's mother's side and shook his head. "You leave that girl alone. She's been shot for cryin' out loud. She don't need you pickin'. Hi, honey. You look great."

"Thanks, Harry." Gloria managed a smile for her new stepfather and glanced back at her mom. "You didn't have to rush up here for this. I'll be heading home soon."

Her mom frowned. "What's soon? You had surgery, hon, you're going to be in here at least another day."

"I know, but that's still soon. You could've taken your time and driven up." Gloria sighed. "I don't mean to sound ungrateful."

"Are you in pain?" Harry reached over and squeezed her hand.

Gloria closed her eyes and focused. "Maybe that's it."

"Push the button then, honey. They give you the medicine for a reason." Her mom pulled a chair closer to the bed and sat. "Then you can tell me all about how things are going with Jonah."

"Jonah? What about him?" Gloria relaxed into the pillows as the pain began to ebb.

"That nice girl, Ruth, she's his sister, right? She was telling us all about how the two of you are finally together. She's happier than a pig in mud about it too, let me tell you." Her mom smiled. "So it was hard to be annoyed that I'm the last to know my daughter's in love."

Did everyone know she was in love with Jonah? Clearly she wasn't any good at masking her emotions, which would've been great to know before she tried to bluff a wanted felon at a traffic stop. "Yes, Mom. I love him and he loves me."

"Oh, how exciting." Her mom's voice came out as a squeal and she clapped her hands several times. "When's the wedding? I understand the two of you have been friends a long time, so surely there's no reason to wait."

Gloria scoffed. "Yeah, try telling him that. I'm not sure how we'll end up at the altar when he won't even kiss me."

"Hmm. Well..." Her mom glanced over at Harry. "Maybe he's one of those boys who doesn't think you should kiss until your wedding day. Seems I recall that being a thing among church people."

"He didn't seem to have any trouble kissing Kenia." Gloria frowned and pushed aside the image of the two of them on the dance floor at Micah and Serena's wedding.

"Who's that? Never mind, doesn't matter." Her mother waved her words away. "You're just going to have to convince him it's the right thing to do. Sometimes men need a little push."

Harry laughed and leaned over to kiss his wife's cheek. "Women do too, sometimes."

Her mother's cheeks pinked. "Yes, well. This is my daughter we're talking about. She's always been a go-getter."

Gloria drooped. She was definitely that. Go-getter. Independent. Aggressive. Unfeminine. Choose the adjective, she'd heard them all. Was it too much to ask that just once in her life a man would want her enough to do the chasing? For two years, Jonah had pursued her when she wasn't free. Now that she was, she'd had to practically beg for each step in a forward direction. "I don't know, Mom. I don't feel like it should be my job. I'm getting tired. Would it be okay if I took a nap?"

"Of course, baby. You close your eyes. Harry and I brought along plenty of things to entertain ourselves." Her mom settled back in the guest chair.

Gloria closed her eyes. Jonah *did* love her. She didn't question that. They'd talked about the divorce and she'd thought she'd convinced him she didn't need more time to heal. So why was he still so hesitant to do something about it?

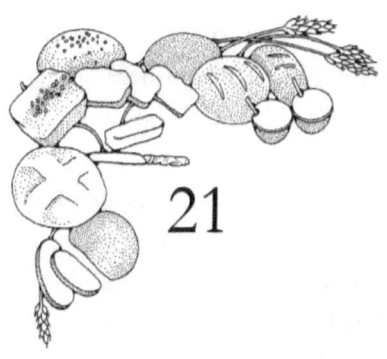

# 21

The dining room at the B&B was crowded and loud. Jonah set the platter holding a stuffed, roasted pork shoulder surrounded by vegetables in the center of the table and headed back toward the kitchen.

"I still don't think you should be doing so much." Jonah took the serving dish out of Ruth's hands. "You just got home."

"I know. But it feels good to be back. Besides, I gave birth two months ago, so it's not like I'm the one who just got out of the hospital." Ruth turned and stirred a pot on the stove. "I'm bummed Gloria won't be released until tomorrow, though. I was hoping she'd be part of our first full family lunch in a while. She *is* going to be family soon, right?"

Jonah's ears burned. It's what he wanted. More than anything. Seeing her in the hospital had driven that home. "I hope so. I figure I need to wait until she's healed, though."

"Oh my goodness." Ruth turned, hands on her hips. "No. You do not need to wait any longer than you already have. You've been friends for three years, seeing each other and talking practically every day. Is there anything you don't know about her?"

He shrugged. "I didn't know she was married. So, maybe?"

"Bzzt. No. The answer is no. Or if there is, it's something that doesn't matter. You've disagreed about things and managed to stay friends. You not only love her, but you like her. Just ask her already."

"You think?"

Ruth nodded. "I know. Grab the salad, I'll get this. Then let's get everyone settled. That pork smells amazing. What did you call it again?"

"*Porchetta*. It's an Italian stuffed pork. It seemed festive. And you and Corban being home is definitely reason to celebrate."

Ruth stood on her tiptoes and pressed a kiss to Jonah's cheek. "Thanks. We're so glad to be home. Did I mention we invited Gloria's mom and stepdad to lunch?"

Jonah froze. "No. You didn't mention that."

"Ah. Well, I did." She grinned over her shoulder at him. "They seem nice."

Maybe since Ruth had already cornered him about his plans for Gloria the rest of the table would leave it alone? Surely between oohing and ahhing over the baby and talking with Ursula about her pregnancy there'd be enough to keep him out of the spotlight? Dragging his feet, he crossed the hall to the dining room and set the last bowls on the table before taking his seat.

"It's so good to be home and back with all of you." Corban reached for Ruth's hand and brought it to his lips. "Why don't I say grace and we can dig in? I think Jonah outdid himself today."

Jonah bowed his head while Corban blessed the food. This was almost perfect. If only Gloria could be here with them. Maybe Ruth was right. It was time to take his foot off the brakes.

"So. When Jonah gets back down here on the planet with us." Everyone chuckled at Corban's words.

Jonah's face heated. "Sorry."

"He'll carve up that pork roast. Everyone else, grab what's closest and pass to the right." Corban grinned and reached for the salad that sat in front of him, dropping a small spoonful on his plate before passing it to Ruth.

"How are you feeling, Ursula?" Ruth took some salad and passed it before fixing her gaze on her sister-in-law. "Any morning sickness?"

Ursula chuckled. "Not really. Maybe a little queasy every now and then, but nothing major."

"Unfair." Ruth shook her head, taking a roll as the basket passed by her. "Maybe it'll come. You're only what, three weeks along?"

"Four." Ursula shrugged. "If it does, so be it. My mom says she was never sick, so maybe I'm going to inherit her good pregnancy genes. Still, it's a long time between now and January."

"It'll be here before you know it." Serena glanced at Micah. "If we're talking about babies, maybe now's the time for us to share some news of our own."

Jonah frowned. Hadn't Serena said she couldn't get pregnant? It had caused a fairly major bump right as they'd gotten engaged. Well, major for her. Micah had never been worried. "News is good."

Serena offered a slight smile. "It's one of those good with the bad things. The movie is, for all intents and purposes, cancelled. I'm still officially attached to the project, but it's not looking like there's going to be a director—or a production company at this point—any time soon."

"That makes my schedule for the next eighteen months easier." Jonah finished slicing the *porchetta* and passed it down the table. "But I'm sorry."

Serena shrugged. "Micah's response was pretty much the same. It's okay. As much as I love the script, without the right director it could end up being a disaster. I really feel like the original director was the best one for the project. But between Ruth giving birth and Ursula getting pregnant, we decided maybe we don't need to wait to start a family. So we're starting to look at adoption agencies."

"Really?" Ruth grabbed Corban's hand. "That makes me so happy. All the cousins growing up together close in age. But what if another movie comes along?"

Micah sipped his water before speaking. "We'll cross that bridge if we get to it. Adoption isn't exactly a fast process, so it might not be an issue. But we're agreed that this is our top priority, so unless the movie is one that she simply can't pass up, that's what we'll do."

Serena nodded.

Harry swallowed the enormous mouthful of food and thumped himself on the chest. "This is some mighty fine food. Thanks for including us when we're nothing to y'all but paying guests. But it sure is nice to know Gloria's found herself a family like yours here in Idaho. Her mama's been hoping she'd move back to Georgia, but I think we both can see that she's right where she belongs, can't we, hon?"

Gloria's mom nodded, dabbing at her eyes with her napkin. "We sure can. And you, Jonah, if you love my girl half as much as I think you do, don't keep her waiting around for you. She's got a powerful need to be loved. She hides it well, but it's there all the same."

Everyone stared down the table at him.

Jonah swallowed. "Yes, ma'am."

Harry laughed and took his wife's hand. "Let the boy alone, Billie May. I don't reckon Gloria would thank you for getting involved. That said, listen to the woman, she knows her daughter. And that girl is worth keeping."

"Yes, sir. That's the plan." At least, it was now. Maybe he was a little thick-skulled sometimes, but enough people said the same thing to him, he could get a clue. Looked like he'd be heading over to Arcadia Valley's local jewelry store, Facets, in the morning. "Apparently, I'm done waiting."

Everyone chuckled.

Jonah smiled and looked around at his family gathered around the table. Yep. The only thing missing was Gloria.

Jonah peeked around the hospital room door as he knocked.

"Come in." Gloria still sounded tired. And maybe a little sad.

"Hey." He frowned and scrutinized her expression. "What's wrong?"

"I have to stay another day. My surgical site isn't healing the way they hoped, so they want to keep an eye on it a little longer. I want to go home."

"I'm sorry." He ignored the box in his pocket. Maybe this wasn't the right time, after all. He glanced at the screen of her tablet as it lay on her lap. "What are you reading?"

Pink tinged her cheeks and she reached for the off button. "Just a poem I memorized in high school."

He lifted his eyebrows. "Who's it by?"

"Shelley. It's...I was thinking of copying it out for you. Probably would have, if I hadn't gotten shot."

"Yeah? Can I see?" He held out a hand for the tablet.

Gloria hesitated before pressing the power button again and swiping to activate the screen and handing it to him.

Jonah glanced at the title. *Love's Philosophy*. Okay. He skimmed the first stanza, his eyebrows knitting together. He kept reading, pausing on the last lines. *What is all this sweet work worth if thou kiss not me?* His eyes flicked up to hers and held them. "I spent a lot of yesterday being told I'm slow and over think things. I take it you'd agree."

Gloria pressed back into the pillows, her cheeks now a fiery red. "Well. I just...yeah, I guess. I love you, Jonah. I want us to be together."

Maybe it was the right time, after all. "You do, huh?"

"I do. If you don't—if you've changed your mind, I wish you'd just tell me." Gloria's good hand balled, gathering a fist full of the sheet.

"As it happens—"

Gloria drew in a quick breath.

Jonah stood, lowered the rail on the side of the hospital bed, and perched beside her. He pried the fingers of her hand away from the covers and held it. "As it happens, I have changed my mind about something. See, I figured you needed more time, regardless of what you said. I didn't want to rush you, or push you, because I didn't want you comparing me to Frank. I know there are places I won't measure up. He was a Marine. I'm just a cook."

"Jonah."

He put a finger to her lips. "I love you. And I'm ready to take you at your word and stop trying to give you space you don't want. Or need."

Gloria swallowed.

Jonah reached into his pocket and withdrew the small square box with the word "Facets" written on it in ornate cursive. He popped open the lid and held it out. "Gloria Sinclair, will you marry me?"

Her mouth formed a little "o" and her eyes filled, tears brimming over to slip down her cheeks. She reached for the box with her good hand and gasped.

Jonah grinned. Since Gloria was a police officer, he hadn't gone for a big, flashy solitaire, but the circle of diamonds had caught his eye. The jeweler had assured him that it wasn't going to catch on anything. "It's called an eternity ring. I thought it was perfect, because that's what I want for us. Eternity."

"Oh, Jonah. Yes. Of course I'll marry you."

He gently took the ring from the box and slid it onto her left hand. "We can get the size fixed—"

"Jonah?"

"Yeah?"

"Shut up and kiss me already."

He chuckled and lowered his lips to hers. "Yes, ma'am."

# Arcadia Valley Romance:
## Six authors. Six series. One community.

Welcome to Arcadia Valley, Idaho, where a foodie culture and romance grow hand-in-hand. Join my friends and me as we release a book every month set in Arcadia Valley. You'll enjoy meeting old friends and making new ones as each of the six authors' books intertwine with the previous stories in this Christian romance series. Get started with Romance Grows in Arcadia Valley and follow along at ArcadiaValleyRomance.com to make sure you don't miss any installments!

www.ArcadiaValleyRomance.com

Joy of My Heart

Romance From The Heart

LEE TOBIN McCLAIN

# Chapter One

Lucas Ruiz Morales hadn't expected a big brass band to greet him, but having someone at least answer the door would have been nice.

He tapped again on the door of his ancestral home in Arcadia Valley, Idaho. Yes, his grandfather had been sick, but where was Connie, his housekeeper? Where were the visiting nurses?

After repeated knocking, Lucas retrieved the key from the spot under a decorative planter where it had always been kept and let himself into the house. Maybe his abuelo was asleep. Lots of older people lost some hearing. Maybe he just hadn't heard the knocking.

He was ashamed he didn't know more about his grandfather's condition. But that was all about to change.

"Belo?" He walked through the sprawling home that his parents, both now gone, had fondly called La Hacienda. When he got to the master bedroom, he saw signs of his grandfather: tangled bedclothes, pill bottles on the nightstand, a large-print library book open, face down beside the pillows.

The man himself was nowhere in sight.

"Belo?" He called louder now and checked the adjoining bathroom. Empty.

The house echoed as he hurried to the big farmhouse kitchen. It was a lonely sound, and guilt stabbed him again. For his grandfather to be rattling around by himself in this giant place wasn't right. Yes,

Lucas had arranged for nursing staff to be there around the clock, but that didn't make up for the lack of family.

And speaking of nurses, where were they? And where was Amiga, Belo's beloved, three-legged corgi mix?

"Hello? Belo? Anyone?" He called louder now, searching the dining room and living area.

He heard a thump.

Lucas cocked his head, seeking the source of the sound. He heard it again. From the basement.

"Belo?" Surely his grandfather couldn't make it down the old house's steep cellar stairs. The man was almost ninety.

But when he checked, a dim light shone from the basement, and there was another thumping sound.

Bracing himself for intruders—because maybe he'd missed a memo and Belo was staying somewhere else, leaving an opportunity for thieves to break in—Lucas made his way down the stairs, hand on the sheathed knife in his pocket. He wasn't a violent man, but you didn't spend a decade as a war correspondent in the most remote, dangerous parts of the world without learning to take care of yourself.

He reached the bottom of the stairs and a shape rose up out of the darkness. He lifted his knife and feinted left, then moved right, and some kind of stick came crashing down where he'd been.

He caught his assailant around the waist.

A small, bony waist. With a familiar, musty-spicy smell. "Belo?"

"So, you have finally arrived," Belo said in his precise, accented English. "Why are you creeping up on me?"

"I thought you had an intruder! Didn't you hear me calling?" He loosened his grip and eased his grandfather over toward the steps. "What are you doing down here, anyway?"

"I am searching out something for you." The old man gestured toward a pile of boxes. He'd obviously been down here awhile, going through them.

His wrinkled hand was ice-cold. Not good. "I can get you whatever you need later," Lucas said. "Come on upstairs."

"Not until I find it." Belo stumped over toward the pile of boxes. "It is in here somewhere. I remember."

"What are you looking for?"

"Mama's necklace." He knelt, awkwardly and slow, and rifled through a box in the dim light. "Make yourself of some use. That blue box—right there—pull it down. You are as tall as a giraffe."

The grumpy words made Lucas grin, but he reached up and pulled down the box his five-foot-six grandfather couldn't possibly have reached. "If you'll tell me what it looks like, I'll help you find it. Is it in a jewelry box?"

"Pouch. Velvet." Belo shoved aside the box he'd been working on and opened the one Lucas had gotten down for him. "Green, I think."

Lucas turned on the flashlight from his phone and shone it into the box. Immediately, he saw a scrap of green velvet. "Is this it?" he asked, extracting it from the heap of papers, ribbons, and china knickknacks.

"At last you have done something useful. Help me up."

That was Belo. If you wanted a bunch of easy compliments, you didn't turn to him. Lucas extended his hand and helped his grandfather to his feet, steadied him, and then shoved the boxes out of the middle of the floor with his foot. "Satisfied now? Can we go upstairs?"

Belo didn't answer, he just led the way. Which was good, because Lucas wanted to walk behind to catch him if he fell.

The old man made it up the stairs, slow step by slow step, and shuffled to the kitchen table, sinking into a chair with a little groan. "Ah, Miho. I'm not as young as I used to be."

Tell me something I don't know. "Where are your nurses?"

"I did not like them," Belo said, "and they did not like me."

Lucas could only imagine.

"So I sent the last one away yesterday. Because you were coming."

Oh, man.

Lucas wasn't sure how long he could stay. His new work as a freelance food-and-health writer wasn't exactly location dependent, but since his assistant was in New York, he based his travels from there.

Automatically, he moved to the old stove and put the kettle on, just as he'd watched his grandmother do so often in the past. He opened and closed cupboard doors, looking for tea, noting with dismay the sticky film on some of the dishes and the lack of supplies. He could barely find a teabag.

"So what happened with Connie?" he asked, as a starting point. Belo's housekeeper had worked here for most of her life and she'd never have left the kitchen in this state.

Belo shrugged. "She had to go take care of her sister. I'm fine. Get these worthless nursing staff to do a little work."

"But... they can't keep up if you've fired them." Lucas opened the refrigerator, which held a carton of milk—expired--a few wilted celery stalks and peppers, and a package of lunch meat. No wonder Belo was getting so thin.

"It doesn't matter. Sit down." Belo's voice was still authoritative, and Lucas was still enough of an obedient grandson that he obeyed.

"I want to talk to you. Give you something." He held up the green velvet pouch with shaking hands and fumbled to open it.

Lucas wanted to grab it away and do it himself, but respect compelled him to let Belo take his time.

Finally, he got the pouch open and extracted a tarnished silver necklace, embedded with turquoise and rose quartz. "Ah, still beautiful." He held it out. "This is for you."

Lucas took it and studied it. "It's a women's necklace. I remember Mama wearing it."

"That's right." Belo nodded. "And now, it is time you found a woman to give it to."

Lucas lifted an eyebrow. "What do you know about women in my life?"

"Only that you don't have them," Belo said with a disgusted snort. "Not enough, anyway. Not one special one."

That was undeniably true, and there was a good reason for it. Lucas stood and went to the stove, checking the gas burner and listening to the water start to boil. "Where's the mutt?" he asked, seeking to change the subject.

"I lost her two months ago." Belo's voice thickened, just a little, and Lucas glanced over and saw the sadness on his grandfather's face.

How lonely the old man must be, without his loyal companion.

But Belo wasn't one to share the softer emotions. He cleared his throat. "There is something I want you to do."

"Oh? What's that?" Lucas was getting a bad feeling. He poured the water over teabags in two cups, even though it wasn't quite boiling. He carried the cups to the table.

Belo put his hands around the outside of the cup but didn't drink it "The time has come for you to marry," he said.

"Oh, really?" Lucas frowned, dunking his tea bag. "Why's that?"

"The Ruiz name dies with you and me," Belo said, "unless we continue it." He flashed a ghost of a smile. "And I haven't met anyone lately."

The weak attempt at a joke, more than anything else, made Lucas sit up and take notice. Belo wasn't usually much for joking.

"What brought this on?" he asked, buying himself time to figure out how to tell Belo what he needed to tell him.

Belo reached out a veined, wrinkled hand and gripped Lucas's forearm with surprising strength. "I have a diagnosis," he said.

A hollow feeling started in Lucas's stomach. "What is it?"

"It's my heart, complications from the diabetes," Belo said. "The odds aren't good."

The hollowness spread to Lucas's chest and throat, making it hard to breathe. He put his hand over Belo's and looked down at it. Two brown hands, one old, one young. Both with the thick fingers and prominent veins of a Ruiz.

They were the last of their line. Could it be true that Belo wasn't long for this world?

No. He didn't accept that. "What doctor told you that?" he asked. "There's nobody here in Arcadia Valley qualified to make that kind of diagnosis."

"The doctors sent me to Twin Falls," he said. "There, I was seen by good doctors."

"Good local doctors, sure." Lucas blew out a sharp breath, his head filling with plans. "We'll set up an appointment at the Carnegie Clinic in Denver. I have a friend I can call—"

"You're not listening." Belo clutched Lucas's arm tighter. "I don't need a big-city doctor. What the Twin Falls Heart Center said was good enough for me, nothing less than what I've sensed myself."

"But Belo—"

"I'm eighty-nine years old and I've had a good life. But this conversation isn't about me." He took up the pendant Lucas had put down and handed it to him again. "I want you to marry and have children. It's time. Before I go, I want to see you settled down here on La Hacienda with a good woman. Preferably pregnant."

Lucas stared at his grandfather. Had the old man lost his mind? "I have a few plans other than finding and impregnating a wife," he said. "Something called a career?"

Belo waved a dismissive hand. "You can write books anywhere. And it does not take so long to find a woman. Why, I met your grandma—"

"I know, at a VA dance, and you married her a month later," Lucas said. He'd heard the story a dozen times.

"And we had a happy life," Belo said. "My one regret is that we only had one child." He looked away, but not before Lucas saw reflected in his eyes the same pain that was in Lucas's heart. His parents. Happy and in love and doing good work one day, dead in a car crash the next, victims of a drunk driver.

"So carrying on the family name is up to you, and you're not getting any younger. What are you, thirty?"

"Thirty six," Lucas admitted reluctantly.

"No hay mucho tiempo. You must find a woman. Polish this before you give it to her." Belo pushed back his chair and stood. "Now, I must go to bed. You make yourself at home and I'll see you tomorrow."

Was this some kind of a joke? "I'm not getting married, Belo."

His grandfather opened his mouth to speak and then closed it. His eyes, more watery than Lucas remembered, and he looked steadily at Lucas.

Then his grandfather shook his head a little and turned away. "I am tired," he said as he headed toward the door. Frailer, maybe even shorter than he'd used to be.

Lucas stared after him, shaking his head. The old man was loco. People didn't get married to continue a family name, not anymore.

But that didn't make Lucas feel any better about disappointing him.

From the hostess stand of El Corazon, Veronica Quintana smiled at the McKennas, parents of a classmate she'd known her whole life. "Thanks for coming tonight," she said, her friendly customer service persona coming back to her, as comfortable as an old pair of jeans.

She'd loved her writing job in Twin Falls—well, most things about it—but, reluctant as she was to admit it, El Corazon was home.

Mrs. McKenna shrugged into the coat her husband held for her. "We love Mexican food! But it's too bad about your job, honey."

"Thought you were running the website for that big newspaper over in Twin Falls," Mr. McKenna boomed, loud enough for the half-full restaurant to hear. "That gig sure didn't last long!"

The smile froze on Veronica's face. "No, it didn't." Three months, to be exact.

Three months of being her own independent woman, until things had gone terribly downhill terribly fast and she'd come home to Arcadia Valley with her tail between her legs.

And while she loved El Corazon, she didn't love the feeling of failure that reared up whenever people asked—or didn't ask, but wanted to—about what had happened to the new job.

"Well, we're glad you're back," Mrs. McKenna said, patting Veronica's shoulder. "It's always nice when our young people stay in Arcadia Valley. And with your family here to take care of you, you can take your time figuring out your next move."

"Or maybe there won't be a next move," Mr. McKenna said. "Nothing wrong with helping out in the family business. Your parents would be glad."

Veronica glanced automatically at the large portrait of her parents on the restaurant's wall. They'd started this place, had loved it, had made it grow. They'd both been excellent cooks with a good sense of what customers wanted.

Whereas Veronica couldn't fry an egg without burning it.

As the couple left the restaurant, Veronica's oldest brother, Javier, strode out of the kitchen and toward the hostess stand. "Heard you come in late last night," he said as he picked up the clipboard to see which tables were still available. "Where were you?" As he spoke, his eyes scanned the restaurant, checking everything out, making sure there wasn't a napkin or fork out of place.

"Yeah, where were you?" her brother Alex called from the other side of the dining room. He wore a white apron and was bussing a table, subbing for an employee who'd called in sick.

She glared at Alex. He was just a couple of years older than she was and should know better than to stick his nose into her business. He was supposed to be on her side against their oldest brother's overprotectiveness.

"It's okay." Her middle brother, Daniel, spoke up from the table where he sat with his twins and his new wife, Tabitha. "She was at Karaoke night at the American Legion. One of my patients mentioned it." He tilted his head to one side as he looked at Veronica. "Did you really sing 'All My Exes Live In Texas?' Twice?"

"I love that song," one of the few remaining customers said, and started to whistle it.

Veronica let her head sink into her hands.

She was twenty-six years old, with a college degree in media and journalism. She'd lived on her own, hosted exchange students, helped to start a women's prayer group. When she'd moved to Twin Falls, she'd made new friends right away. She'd started volunteering at an animal rescue farm and singing in the church choir.

And then everything had blown up around her. Her confidence had been shaken, her sense of herself as a professional—and as a woman—chopped down.

And now here she was, back in Arcadia Valley, living with her brother and his wife. And having her every movement scrutinized by not just Javier, but her two other brothers and half the rest of the town as well.

She had to get out of here. To lick her wounds, to regain her self-assurance, to start over.

"You boys leave Veronica alone." Daniel's wife, Tabitha, came over to put an arm around her. "She's a grown woman, and it's nobody's business what she sings at the Legion!"  She lifted an eyebrow at Veronica. "Although I wish you had better taste. Country music… ugh."

Alex slipped over and changed up the music station from Latin contemporary to wailing country. When Tabitha glared at him, he laughed. "Just want to bother my newest sister-in-law," he said.

"Veronica will always be my baby sister," Javier said. "And I don't like the idea of you staying late at the Legion, hermanita. Most of the folks there are good people, but you never know—"

"Thanks for your concern." She was going for sarcasm, but it fell flat.

Because the truth was, as much as she railed against it, a part of her did like her brothers' concern. Wasn't that why she'd come running back to Arcadia Valley?

"Come on, let's have some girl talk." Tabitha pulled Veronica out of her seat. "The rush is over, and your brothers can handle whoever's left."

Veronica followed her friend to a corner table, grabbing a basket of chips and a cup of salsa from the stand beside the kitchen. "Is it just me, or are they amazingly overprotective?"

"It's not just you." Tabitha laughed. "Daniel's the least overbearing, but even he can get bossy when it's a question of family. But they mean well."

"They do. I know they do. It's just… I got a taste of freedom living in Twin Falls. When I came back, everything started to feel different." She sighed. "Seems like they didn't grate on me as much before."

"Well, you weren't living with Javier and Molly before," Tabitha said. "Living at the cottages gave you at least a little bit of freedom. Do you want to come stay with Daniel and me and the girls?"

Veronica crunched a chip. "You're sweet. But I'm not going to be a third wheel with you newlyweds."

Tabitha snorted, looking over at the table where Daniel was wiping up a drink one of the twins had spilled. "It's not like we have a lot of privacy anyway, with the twins around."

Daniel glanced over their way, and when he noticed Tabitha looking at him, his lips turned up at the corners.

Their gazes locked, and it seemed to Veronica that the temperature in the dining room went up by ten degrees.

"Daddy! Can we have flan for dessert?" one of the twins asked. Daniel got involved in that discussion, and Tabitha looked back at Veronica, a faraway look in her eyes and a smile lingering on her lips. "What were we… oh. Yeah. You'd totally be welcome to stay with us. We'd love to have you."

That was all she needed, to watch Tabitha and Daniel fall ever more deeply in love when she'd ruled that out for herself. "Thanks, but no. What I need is my own place."

At least, until she could scrape together the money to leave Arcadia Valley.

"You can't get your cottage back?"

Veronica shook her head. "No. Those places are in high demand, since there aren't many rental properties around." She sighed. "I feel like I'm going backward in my life, you know? All I want is to stand on my own two feet and be independent."

"I hear you," Tabitha said sympathetically. And she wasn't faking sympathy, but Veronica couldn't miss the way her eyes flickered toward Daniel again.

All three of her brothers had found love in the past two years. They'd all settled down and were living their adult lives.

Only Veronica was still wandering, acting like a kid, staying out and singing Karaoke, which, for the record, hadn't even been that much fun, since she'd been one of the few sober customers in the place.

The bells on the front doors jingled. "That's my cue," she said to Tabitha. She walked up to the hostess stand, glancing at the clock on the wall. Eight forty-five, so the kitchen was open for another fifteen minutes. And it had been drilled into her by her parents: treat the last customer just as well as you'd treat the first. "One for dinner?" she asked, picking up the menu.

Only then did she look closely at the customer. Hair cropped as close as a military man, brown eyes, muscles to die for. He was familiar, and yet not.

"Take out," the man said. Then he did a double take. "Veronica? Veronica Quintana?"

From three separate points in the room, her brothers' dark heads swiveled toward the newcomer.

"I'm Veronica." She studied him, trying to keep an impassive expression as her insides jumped and danced. "Do we know each other?"

# Books in the Arcadia Valley Romance Series

## Want a Free Book?

If you enjoyed Donuts & Daydreams and would like to read another of my books for free, you can get a free e-book simply by signing up for my newsletter here: http://bit.ly/2g0AGvf

## Author's Note

Thank you for reading Donuts & Daydreams! I hope that you enjoyed it! I'm sad to be leaving Arcadia Valley behind as this book marks the end of my Baxter Family Bakery series. I spent many a joyful hour with the Baxters and they will forever hold a little piece of my heart. I know I'll be looking for a way to give them a cameo here and there in future books, if only so we can check-in and make sure their happily ever afters are progressing as they should.

I would appreciate it if you'd help others enjoy it too by leaving a review! Word of mouth is how most people say they find new books to read, so I'd love it if you'd also consider telling your friends about it. Any success my books have is owed to readers like you who take the time to tell others about my stories. Thank you, from the bottom of my heart.

Working on this project, with the five other amazing authors who are all writing in Arcadia Valley, has been an absolute delight. I love all the characters who fill up our little town, and I hope you will, too. Each of the ladies who are a part of Arcadia Valley has a great talent and a deep love for Christian fiction. I think you'll agree it shows in the work they produce.

You can always keep up to date with my writing news via my newsletter. There's a sign-up form at my website http://bit.ly/2g0AGvf and also on my author Facebook page

http://www.Facebook.com/ElizabethMaddrey.

I continue to owe a huge debt of gratitude to my husband and sons for giving me the time to write, my sister for her unflinching support and encouragement, and my critique partners Valerie Comer, Lynellen Perry, Heather Gray and Jan Elder for catching all the times I use the same word six times in two paragraphs.

More than anything, I'm grateful that God continues to give me words and makes it possible for me to write them down.

I'd love to hear from you! You can connect with me on Facebook my webpage or via email.

# About the Author

Elizabeth Maddrey began writing stories as soon as she could form the letters properly and has never looked back. Though her practical nature and love of computers, math, and organization steered her into computer science at Wheaton College, she always had one or more stories in progress to occupy her free time. This continued through a Master's program in Software Engineering, several years in the computer industry, teaching programming at the college level, and a Ph.D. in Computer Technology in Education. When she isn't writing, Elizabeth is a voracious consumer of books and has mastered the art of reading while undertaking just about any other activity.

Elizabeth is the author of more than fifteen books, both fiction and non-fiction. She lives in the suburbs of Washington, D.C. with her husband and their two incredibly active little boys.